Advance Praise for *Jacket Weather*

"Poetic and compulsively readable, *Jacket Weather* invents a new genre—call it lyrical realism. Mike DeCapite casts a cool but affectionate eye on New York in the 2010s, as it lives on despite having become a replica of itself. Like Virginie Despentes's *Vernon Subutex*, *Jacket Weather* traces the lives of those who've stayed on after the party. It's a love story improbably set at the beginning of late middle age, and it's also a story of cities, survival, adaptation, desire, and a celebration of the small pleasures we invent and discover to offset unavoidable loss."
—CHRIS KRAUS, author of
I Love Dick and *After Kathy Acker*

"*Jacket Weather* describes in exacting detail what daily life looks like when you see it through the lens of romantic love. Every scrap of talk and every sign on the street is irradiated by love—and its step-sibling, anxiety. The book is funny, tender, often exhilarating, and borne aloft by DeCapite's ardent, plainspoken lyricism. You can't stop reading it."
—LUC SANTE, author of
Low Life and *Maybe the People Would Be the Times*

"Mike DeCapite's books all feel like movies to me. The characters, and the rooms and seasons they inhabit, are clear before my eyes. For example, if anyone should ask me to describe the goings-on at the YMCA, I feel expert on the

subject. Not that I've ever been in a Y, but from reading De-Capite's novels and short stories, I've spent a good amount of time there. I know the ins and outs of the Ys in Cleveland, San Francisco, and New York City. I know that in these YMCA locker rooms around the country, naked men are standing around talking at length (and quite hilariously) about the preparation of pork cutlets, meatballs, and sauces. The other thing I've learned from reading DeCapite's work is that love is a messy business. As surely as there will be sweaty weight rooms there will be ruined marriages swapped out for doomed romance. The losses are crushing. However, here in *Jacket Weather*, Mike has finally found June. Sure she's married but that's beside the point. In this case, Mike writes about a more matured, lasting love. The love is both for June and for New York City. I hope he isn't jinxing anything." —KELLY REICHARDT, director of *Wendy and Lucy* and *First Cow*

"*Jacket Weather* is a tender love story that blossoms like a rose in the concrete of a city always on the verge. DeCapite's effortless prose stirs echoes of certain New York School poets, of 'cold rosy dawn in New York City,' night streets illuminated by great bars and the music streaming out of them, the endless possibilities of a place where, despite persistent evidence to the contrary, 'love is the heart of everything.'"
—MAX BLAGG, author of *Slow Dazzle* and *Loud Money*

"I don't think there exists another novel like *Jacket Weather*. Mike DeCapite has flawless pitch for dialogue and an imagist's eye, and his prose is lucent and uncluttered, but what's really a surprise (and should not be) is this: he's written an almost unbearably tender love story for adults. The days and weeks and seasons and every quotidian detail vibrate with newness and suspense."

—MIMI LIPSON, author of *The Cloud of Unknowing*

"Mike DeCapite has an eye for deep beauty in the mundane. He writes prose that makes poetry of just walking down the street. What he observes injects a charged current into life's moments between. Reading *Jacket Weather* is like listening to the world reveal its secrets."

—ROBERT GORDON, author of
It Came from Memphis and *Respect Yourself:*
Stax Records and the Soul Explosion

"In this roman à clef—minus the clef—I can clearly hear the music of the NYC streets, feel the L train as it hums, and can smell something cookin'—a modern *Moveable Feast*."

—CLINTON HEYLIN, author of
The Double Life of Bob Dylan and
From the Velvets to the Voidoids:
The Birth of American Punk Rock

"This could *almost* be a young man's account of a life and a love, *almost* a collection of youthful journal entries, but it's clearly not. The gravitas of *age* permeates these artful, observant pages. Mike DeCapite has been around, has *seen* things, including all the ways we attempt to come together, and all the ways we will always remain apart. Love under the weight of age reads quite differently from young love, and is not often this well portrayed. *Jacket Weather* is chock full of living, of years spent noticing the streets at dusk as the lights turn from green to red and people make their crosswalk migrations and sometimes attempt small connections, to relate a thought or observation, tryin' to tell a vision.

"This is a beautiful, evocative account of a late-in-life love sprung into being in early twenty-first-century Manhattan, characters tossed forth from the aftermath of the punk rock seventies. Protagonist Mike spins cryptic, poetic observations of his daily life, strikes random and true chords, pen as Telecaster. His plaintive adoration of June, the love of his life, is painted with enduring mystery and great respect. I loved this book." —LEE RANALDO, Sonic Youth, author of *Road Movies* and *jrnls80s*

Praise for *Through the Windshield*

"One of the better American novels published in the past several years." —HARVEY PEKAR, *The Austin Chronicle*

"Ravishing . . . One of the reasons Ed's stories are so great is DeCapite's gift for dialogue. Conversations here are full of partial words and creative punctuation that artfully capture the pattern of the characters' speech. The reader can hear every intonation, see every look."

—BARBARA SCHULTZ, *San Francisco Chronicle*

"Read it for its humor. Read it for its pain. Or read it for its language, a hard-boiled version of Beat expansiveness. One thing's certain: with all the different and sometimes contradictory things that this book accomplishes, you'll never read anything else like it."

—FRANK GREEN, *Cleveland Free Times*

"DeCapite's achievement is so extraordinary that a belated appreciation must be penned . . . [A] Whitmanesque hymn . . . *Through the Windshield* triumphs by being about watching, listening, capturing for posterity, eulogizing life and 'leaving the headlights off, so as not to disturb that shadow.'" —JOCKO WEYLAND, *Rain Taxi*

Praise for *Creamsicle Blue*

"The same night I finished *Creamsicle Blue*, I dreamt that some non-existent jacket copy said the book was like a 'soulfriend' . . . Whether he knows it or not, he writes for me, the reader, naming things I've felt but rarely articulated . . . I felt while reading *Creamsicle Blue* that I was experiencing the gradual recognitions and awarenesses that come from the folding-together of thinking, feeling, writing, and living. That is, sometimes life and writing can seem like two parallel realms—but writing about one's life with a clean enough motivation (considering life as lived and felt) can change both the life and the writing and become a third realm . . . Following the uncharted, DeCapite forges a path found only by writing in the quietest moments, by paying attention to the silences in between words and events, and by walking around his city, struggling with the unsayable."

—KAREN LILLIS, Karen the Small Press Librarian

Praise for *Radiant Fog*

"This is a book that will prompt you to head out and take a walk through your city and a book, one better, that will help you see and feel that city in a new way."

—SPENCER DEW, *decomP*

Jacket Weather

ALSO BY MIKE DECAPITE

Through the Windshield
Sitting Pretty
Creamsicle Blue
Radiant Fog

Jacket Weather

a novel

Mike DeCapite

Soft Skull
New York

The author wishes to thank the editors of the following publications,
where excerpts of *Jacket Weather* have appeared in slightly different form:
Local Knowledge, *No Tokens*, *Poetrybay*, and *Vanitas*.

The author gratefully acknowledges reprinting lyrics from
the following songs:
"Breakin' in My Heart" © 1978 by Tom Verlaine
"Rama Lama Ding Dong" © 1958 by George "Wydell" Jones Jr. and
Jimbo Publishing
"Cry Baby" © 1994 by the Waldos and Walter Lure

Library of Congress Cataloging-in-Publication Data
Names: DeCapite, Michael, 1962– author.
Title: Jacket weather : a novel / Mike DeCapite.
Description: First Soft Skull edition. | New York : Soft Skull Press, 2021.
Identifiers: LCCN 2020057121 | ISBN 9781593766931 (paperback) | ISBN
9781593766948 (ebook)
Subjects: LCSH: Middle-aged persons—Fiction. | Music trade—Fiction. |
New York (N.Y.)—Fiction. | GSAFD: Love stories.
Classification: LCC PS3554.E17746 J33 2021 | DDC 813/.54—dc23
LC record available at https://lccn.loc.gov/2020057121

Cover design & Soft Skull art direction by www.houseofthought.io
Book design by Wah-Ming Chang

Published by Soft Skull Press
1140 Broadway, Suite 706
New York, NY 10001
www.softskull.com

Printed in the United States of America
1 3 5 7 9 10 8 6 4 2

I saw the color that sent the geese south
TOM VERLAINE

I've got a girl named
Rama Lama Lama Lama Ding Dong
GEORGE "WYDELL" JONES JR.

Jacket Weather

Standing on the corner, ringing my bell. Here comes Nile, crossing 14th Street. Blazing hot outside, we move over by the bank.

She says "Hey Cleveland, guess who I just ran into? June."

"No kidding."

I never see Nile, but when I do, I ask about June. For years now. She never has any information.

Now she says "I was crossing Twenty-Third Street and she was on the other side, waiting for me. We should get dinner."

•

I slide the gate open with a crash and climb out over South 2nd Street, Williamsburg. It turns out there are heads of Apollo above my windows, and the putty's dirty around the frames. There's a big white rooster in the pigeon coop across the way. Rust has seeped through the crackled paint of the fire escape.

I like the view from the middle of the air, the urban canopy. The mysterious thrill of a streetlight seen too close, too big, as in a dream. The way some convergence of shadows on a window ledge makes it a *place*, or the relationship between the leaves and a projecting sign seems to define an area. There's a liquor-store sign around the corner that's too big for its height from the sidewalk. I want to be up there, near the sign, or in the shadow it throws on the building. To inhabit it, somehow. I see these as places to live. Right? Even though it's only from a distance that they're places. *I want to live on that ledge.* Or *I could see myself on one of those art deco lighting towers near the entrance to the Lincoln Tunnel.* Or *How long could I go unnoticed in a guard box on the Manhattan Bridge?*

Climbing back in the window, I notice how much louder it is out there, even with nothing going on. It's the roar of infinity.

•

I saw June right after I moved back from San Francisco. In Union Square subway. I was with my girlfriend and we got separated going up the stairs, and there was June. She stopped. I stopped. We were ten feet apart. The crowd's going by. It's twenty years since we saw each other. I figured she doesn't recognize me because I used to have long hair.

Or she heard so much about me from my ex-wife she doesn't like me anymore. Later I found out she didn't have her glasses. Anyway, she walked. Lucky my girlfriend missed the whole thing, because I was rattled.

•

Philly comes into the locker room, he opens with "So what's gonna happen? Where we gonna go, when we die? Do we go to heaven? Do we go to sleep? So many questions, not enough answers. Harold, don't lose hope. Patsy, Frank Sinatra's dead. I hate to break it to ya. But he went to heaven, that's the good news. He's with Georgie Jessel."

•

Upstairs, the treadmills face the street. The red vertical Salvation Army sign bounces above the panels of pebbled glass, and a sapling at the curb has gotten its leaves. I cool off walking around the indoor track. Someone's bellowing "Volare." Down below, twenty heavyset elderly women are ranged along one of the lanes of the swimming pool, squiggly black lines at the bottom and white snakes of light slithering on the surface. They're doing their Saturday morning water exercises in their swim caps, bouncing their great big breasts on the water.

·

Philly comes out on the track. I point to my iPod and say "Ray Barretto."

He says "I met Ray Barretto!" We move off to the side, he says "I'm at this club, everybody's in the bathroom doing coke, I see Ray Barretto at a table. And he was the nicest cat! I said 'Ray, baby—remember *Acid*?' 'Cause he did this record called *Acid*. And he kinda laughed, like 'Yeah, I remember acid.'"

Philly starts talking about Johnny Pacheco, the Fania All-Stars, Joe Cuba, Joe Bataan. He's clicking his fingers, he's singing.

He says "I can dance a little bit, so I used to go dancing at the Village Gate, a couple of buddies and me—they called us the Jewbans, because there were a few of us Jewish guys who were into Cuban music. I was never into the rock thing. When I was in high school I heard 'I Wanna Hold Your Hand' and said 'I wanna *hold your hand*'? Gimme a break! This is the squarest shit I ever heard! And from then on, all anybody cared about was the guitar, and everybody sounded the same. They ruined everything! But while everyone else was going to see rock bands, we were going dancing at Roseland and up in Harlem and down on Bleecker Street. One night I'm at a club and I see Machito in there. He was an old cat by then, he'd been around since the forties.

He was it, man. He started the whole thing. So I go up to him—that was the thing about the Latin guys: you could talk to them! Not like the rock guys: you couldn't get anywhere near them. So here comes Machito, and I stand in front of him, I give him a little of my bullshit, y'know—'Machito! The one and only! The *King* of Afro-Cuban Music! Number one!' Right? 'Numero uno! El primero!' And he stops. Because he pinned me, right? And he looks at me, he says—'*Vus machsta?*'"

"[*Laughter*]"

"'*Machen a lebn,*' I told him. 'Making a living.'"

•

Six months later in Whole Foods I saw June again. And again I was there with this girlfriend. There was no Whole Foods in Brooklyn so we used to go to Union Square. It was right before Thanksgiving, June was over by the greens. You know the momentary alarm you feel when it's not you moving backward but the other train moving forward? Time didn't stop, but I stopped and time kept moving past me. I thought *I could walk out of here and follow her anywhere. I would marry her right now.* Partly it was this miserable situation I was in. I was so on edge with this girlfriend I'd be sitting across from an old Polish woman on the subway thinking *She looks nice. Kind. I could trust her.* June didn't see me at Whole Foods. She had a list, and I could tell she was out of her depth. She looked very much alone. And again I didn't speak to her. Would have been nothing but trouble.

Then it's almost three years I don't see her before I run into Nile.

•

R
O
S
E in red neon, a pair of sneakers hanging from the moon. Sitting on the bench outside Atlas, the coffee shop, in the warm night. The traffic signal goes yellow to red to green on parked cars, on the phone box, in the gutter puddle.

A cab rolls up, window down. Cicada sound of its receipt dispenser. Nothing's right anymore, nothing's much good. Maybe it never was. Hank Williams *told* me this forty years ago: you'll never get out of this world alive. Did I think it was just a funny song, or he was just singing about himself?

•

When I walked in on Thursday, Lou was sitting at his locker, still red from the steam. He had three cans of coffee for me, in exchange for the magazines I'd been taking him from work. Every week I took him five copies of *People* and *Entertainment Weekly* and he gave them to women on his rounds. I didn't want anything for them but he was Italian, so he enjoyed transactions. He was at the age when a person starts putting things aside for people and carrying them around in bags: pieces of interest clipped from newspapers and coupons and canned tomatoes. Come to think of it, so was I, with these magazines. This is how it starts.

I thanked him for the coffee and went to my locker.

"Where'd you eat, this weekend?" he said from his row. "Where'd you go?"

"Nowhere: I cooked."

"What'd you make, pasta fazool?"

"No, I made linguine with clams."

"The red?"

"No, the white."

"What'd you do?" he said.

I made my way to the end of the row.

I said "I softened a shallot in oil. I put red pepper flakes."

"Parsley?" he said.

"Yeah, parsley, oregano, then half a cup of white wine, and the juice from the clams."

"You used the canned? What'd you buy, Snow's?"

"Cento."

"Aw, you bought the clam *sauce*?"

"No, the chopped clams."

"I didn't know they made that. I'll have to look for that."

"Yeah. So I put those in about a minute before I drained the pasta, and squeezed some lemon juice."

Lou frowned, approving. He was applying his facial cream. We were naked, this whole time.

I went back to my locker and got into my gear. I said "What about you? Where'd you go?"

"I cooked."

"Yeah? What'd you make?"

"Linguine with clams."

"The white?"

"No, I made the red this time. With the whole baby clams from the can."

"What kind?"

"Doxey's," he said. "What kind of linguine did you buy?"

"Barilla," I said. "You?"

"De Cecco. That's good pasta."

"De Cecco's great, but it's two fifty a box."

"They got it Western Beef, dollar a box."

•

Spring thunder, one a.m. All these bare-bulb windows hanging this way and that in the rain. A yellow, a pink, two blues. In the morning, the lights are still on in two rooms across the street. Man, am I glad I no longer live in rooms where the light stays on all night.

•

That Friday I met them for dinner, Nile and June. Funny place in Chelsea Market, half restaurant, half clothing store. June shows up in a trench coat—*BAM*: big curls, big smile, red lipstick, green eyes—grabs me by the shoulders and kisses me on the mouth and sits down starts talking about she's getting a divorce, selling the apartment, can't wait to get her life back, can't wait to be free and a-*lone*.

•

I never saw her dressed so uptown. I knew her in the eighties, when she was working for Jane Friedman, who used to manage Patti Smith and Candy Darling and Holly Woodlawn but also did press for bands, including my friend Tony's band, Pere Ubu. In those days June's life was all about rock and roll. From record release to club to cab to club to afterparty: black biker jacket, black leggings and boots, and a mass of blueblack curls. For me, she was the living night— all the glamour and potential of a New York night when you're 25. She took people as they came, without judgment. She looked right in your eyes and took you more seriously than you admitted to taking yourself. She surprised you with her interest. And here she was with a raincoat over the back of the chair talking about getting a divorce and saying she's done with relationships. Her ice-calm eyes are the same, the same her glory of curls.

•

We're there about four hours. Then we walk Nile home, and I walk June home in the mist. We wind up under the scaffolding on 16th Street, out of the rain, talking about the prison of being with someone and the release of getting free. She's starting to imagine it. I recommend a book of Vivian Gornick essays I just read, *Approaching Eye Level*, about the pleasures and satisfactions of living alone, for a woman especially, and especially in New York City. June's putting the title in her phone and it's wet below the scaffold and there's a lot more to say, so she invites me up.

•

So I go up, she gets changed. She makes a pot of tea. We get talking about the different things we've been through since the early nineties and how you lose yourself and even good things go stale. We're at their table under a ceiling fixture— that last-call of every kitchen where you've sat up late with people drinking, except I'm not drinking and she's only had a glass of wine all night. Her husband's not around. He works in a restaurant, they barely cross paths.

•

She gets a text from her friend Steph, who's just off a tour with her band, Lez Zeppelin. All-girl band doing Zeppelin. Steph's the Jimmy Page. June's supposed to meet her at the Cubbyhole, on West 4th. So we walk over.

•

Place is packed—we wedge ourselves into the window corner. Steph's talking about the tour. The whole band quit and she's auditioning new people. "Don't Stop Believin'" comes on, loud, and it's like everyone's been waiting all night to hear that song. There's a shift in the room, the crowd pulls together. It's that opening "Chopsticks" figure: kind of a stairway to the stars. We're entering the realm of pure imagination. And then half the bar is singing along, whether ironically or nostalgically or because it's what was playing when *The Sopranos* went black or it's just okay to like that song now I don't know. I'm captivated by its total falsity—its comprehensive pretension—the striving of this suburban jackass with feathered hair to convey some kind of hazy urban fantasy with these counterfeit images: "the midnight train," "a smoky room," "the boulevard." South Detroit? The song seems like it was written by someone who's never been outside. Don't stop believin' in what? Don't lose *what* feeling? Its meaninglessness is like the sky: it goes on and on and on and on. This is what's happened to New York: a bar full of people who brought the suburbs with them, punching the air. June and Steph don't notice, they're talking about something else.

Anyway, that stupid song will always remind me of that night.

•

Talking about it later, June said "Everything was new. In my marriage I was alone, all the time. I was totally on my own. So that night I felt like I was living. I was myself, and I was hanging out with my friends. I felt single, I felt free, I felt seen. Everything was like a discovery and shiny and new. It was like the windows were wide open in my house. This is where I belonged. In the world."

•

I went out to smoke a cigarette. They could see me through the glass. When I went back in, Steph was at the bar. June said "She thinks you're cute." She was still on her first scotch on the rocks, but she was a little lit. "And I agree," she said, and laughed, and knocked into me.

•

Lez Zeppelin had a show coming up in Asbury Park. I told June we should drive down, rent a car, and she said from now on she's not saying no to anything. I walked her back home in the rain. She slid on the wet sidewalk, I caught her arm. When I got down to the L platform it was 3:30. First time *that's* happened in a while.

•

Locker room, the guys are talking about La Maganette.

Philly points at Hector: "*He* was there! Every Wednesday!"

Hector's a trim old guy with a full head of white hair and every hair in place, still wears a gold chain. Keeps to himself. Looks like he knows a few sweet secrets.

"The King of the Mambo!"

Hector gets himself turned around in his white socks and A-shirt and gives me a nod—he's forced to admit it. "They had a Latin dance night," he says.

"And they had a great band," Philly says. "Charanga! Orquesta Broadway."

Hector agrees.

"Where was it?"

"Fiftieth and Third," Lou puts in.

"Mob joint?"

"They all were."

"Just a club, or restaurant too?"

"Italian restaurant upstairs," Lou says. "Downstairs they had dancing."

"It was different every night," Philly says. "Friday was soul dance night. Jake LaMotta used to sit at the bar with a cowboy hat."

"Sit upstairs, in a cowboy hat, with a cigar," Lou confirms. "He's still alive, Jake LaMotta. All the shots he took. Still got all his marbles. Born July 10, 1922. Married seven times."

"You met him on *Raging Bull*?"

Lou has had bit parts in half a dozen mob movies.

"I knew him before. From Times Square, the Metropole, a strip club, he's the bouncer, I used to go see him. Mean! Mean guy. Didn't want nothing to do with nobody, never smiled. Then later I saw him on *Raging Bull*. He still owes me fifty bucks, from a card game."

•

Monday I'm outside One Time Warner, at Columbus Circle, late rush hour, leaning on a post. June does events up there. This afternoon she called to ask if I want to walk her home from work, so I rode the train from Brooklyn. People pouring out of the building, I'm wondering what I'm looking at here. Riding it. I've said it before, I'll say it again: something in us wants action. No matter the danger, no matter the trouble, uproar, or damage. The imp on his throne in the back of your mind, he's always setting you up, putting things in motion. You're telling yourself there's nothing to this, it's two old friends. The imp fidgets. He doesn't care that you've sworn off entanglements and re-claimed your precious time, he's bored with your maxims and regimens—he wants a story. Right now I'm just trying to be here, I'm scanning the people—everything takes so much longer than you imagine and then *wham*, here she is: bright eyes, big smile, dressed for the corporate tower. She takes me back upstairs to show me where she works—I'm walking behind her, watching those Rockette legs . . .

•

And then we're walking down Ninth Avenue, through Hell's Kitchen—part neighborhood, part hallway—people going home, picking up dry cleaning, heading out, all part of what the streets let go of, late in the day. With the heat. Over to Eighth, getting reacquainted, sky bright, streets in shadow, realizing we don't know that much about each other, leaves streaming on the breeze, JESUS SAVES, playground full of kids, the Actors' Temple, woman on a stoop with a plastic tumbler. I was hearing June's story: growing up in Canarsie, yanked out to the island at 15, back and forth between a hospital job and a job at the Ritz, and her lucky break falling under Jane's notice. "We lived on coke and cigarettes and lots of black coffee, we were working with every hot band, and for five minutes we owned New York." She says if Jane hadn't taken her in she'd have wound up turning tricks or dead.

We stopped at Uncle Nick's near the main post office. For some reason I wasn't hungry, I asked the guy for a carton. I carried it five blocks with us before I put it in the trash. Then we made our way down through Chelsea toward the L, trying to make it last.

•

So, to recap. I met them on a Friday. June shows up saying she's done with marriage, done with romance, from here on out she's on her own. I felt the same. I, in fact, was in the middle of writing a *manifesto* about the quiet thrills of solitude. So we stayed up till three in the morning talking about that, self-reliance, keeping the hell out of relationships. Monday she called and asked if I wanted to walk her home from work. Columbus Circle to 14th Street, 45 blocks.

So we did that. And then I had to hurry home and finish my manifesto.

·

For three days, I didn't eat, didn't sleep—I was living on the qui vive, boys. Storms that week, and by night I lay there doing the mental equivalent of shallow breathing, then got up and wandered from room to room naked and starving with a towel around my waist, smoking cigarettes and talking to myself like King Lear, while lightning flashed and thunder cracked and the rain ran off the awnings of the bodegas. All in all, a nervous week.

·

I wrote to my friend Tere—out in San Francisco—who'd counseled me in all weathers.

"I feel crazy. Dizzy, frightened, strange. I can't tell if I'm making all this happen or if I'm kidding myself that I have any control at all. It's like a tab of acid coming on. Or like being drafted. I don't know if I can handle this, T. Overnight, she's my only way to breathe. Why do we *do* this?"

·

There must have been a time when it was possible to see this as the renewal of a friendship. There must have been a day when I was just a little buzzed and happy. Before the—you know—*agonizing transformation* began. But I don't remember it.

•

Philly came in this morning in yellow pants and a Hawaiian shirt with the papers under his arm.

"Dja hear the news, Patsy? Frank Sinatra's still dead!"

He asked what I was listening to. I told him Tappa Zukie.

"Tryna get the spring back in my step," I said.

He said "Who is it?"

"Tapper Zukie."

The name didn't register.

"Reggae guy. Dub."

He said "I once took a girl to the Reggae Lounge."

"On Canal Street."

"I took a woman there named Madeline Silver. She was beautiful! She had beautiful red hair, she had"—he pointed at his cheekbones—"little freckles! Came from the richest Jews in Brooklyn, but she quit them! They disowned her. She was a real lefty. Took her to the Reggae Lounge. Every song sounded the same. I went to the DJ, I said 'Don't you got any James Brown?' He said 'No, we don't do that here.'

I took her once to Fat Tuesday to see Larry Harlow. Remember him? Latin bandleader. They called him El Judio Maravilloso."

"The Marvelous Jew."

"The Wonderful Jew, yeah. He was great. Anyway, took Madeline Silver to see him. Then after, I walked her through the park, tried to kiss her, she said 'No, that's not gonna happen. We're just friends.' So that was the end of that story. I never saw her again. And years later, I went to a party in Brooklyn, I ran into one of her friends, and what do you think happened?"

"She died," I said.

"I asked this woman what ever happened to Madeline Silver, she said 'You didn't hear? She killed herself.' I couldn't believe it. She had everything to live for! I couldn't *believe* it. She lived in those buildings at Prince and Sixth Avenue with the benches out front? She lived on the top floor. I still think about her every time I walk past there."

•

And here comes another chorus of rain. Lightning, voices, laughter. I roll around, I get up and move across the windows in a blanket like some crazy hermit. Whatever room I go into, this thing is true. The rain trickles out, it's over. And here it comes again.

•

To Tere: "I told myself I wouldn't write to June today unless I heard from her, but finally I wrote anyway, just to ask how she was doing, about 1:00. Like a drunk who tells himself he's okay because he hangs on till 1 p.m. before he hustles down to the corner for a half pint of Popov."

•

No solid food since the few smelts I ate at Uncle Nick's. Day and night I feel like throwing up. It's Soup Week, here at Mike's House of Insomnia. In the cafeteria at work, I manage to get down a little broth. Just to settle my stomach. I'm leaving all that behind anyway, the physical realm. Transmuting to pure awareness.

•

Thursday she calls, says she needs to talk to me. She meets me at a reading at Telephone Bar and when it's over we go up the street to Little Poland. I order soup.

Guess what?

So does she.

•

I still see her poking cautiously into the back room at Telephone Bar, trying to slip in unnoticed, shy about intruding.

•

In a booth at Little Poland, she says "I have to talk to you. I can't let myself get involved. I've got too much going on: I have to sell my apartment, I have to separate from my husband and get a divorce, and I need for it to be clean. I don't want to stop seeing you. I've always had a thing for you—twenty years ago I had a thing for you. I was nervous to be around you because you're a writer, I just thought you're so smart, you were the coolest thing, but you were married. Now I'm getting divorced, I need to be there for my divorce. I need to feel it and go through it, and I need to take my heart back and have my own life again."

"Maybe someday" would be easy to say, but she doesn't say it. For everyone's sake she doesn't say it.

She says "I don't know who I am anymore, I need to figure that out. I don't want to stop seeing you—I'm so excited I feel like I'm sixteen. Every morning I go out of my way to walk past the Y, hoping I catch a glimpse of you. I hate the thought of not seeing you. But I realize it might be too hard. I'm being very honest with you. If we have to stop seeing each other, I totally understand."

·

And that's that. She said it, I listened, and now we want dessert. We walk down to Veselka. A little relieved, a little jumpy, as if we've disabled an alarm.

·

Veselka's packed, we sit at the counter. She's talking about growing up. She hated her parents for taking her out of Brooklyn. "I hated everything about Long Island—the trees, the sky, the grass. I just never fit in." The sound of the crickets was the sound of all of that. She lay awake listening to them and then dreamed about escaping with her kid brother in the family car. Her father was a hard case, her mother wanted to keep the peace. They were Old World people—Jews who escaped Germany and Poland: June was a mystery to them. As a teenager, she started coming into the city with five bucks in her pocket—round trip on the Long Island Rail Road, the subway, and a slice—and going to the Palladium.

"How'd you get in?"

"The way it started was it was pissing with rain, and I was with Merri, we were going to see Hot Tuna at the Palladium. Because that's all I listened to growing up in Brooklyn was Hot Tuna. And we didn't have any money for tickets, and Merri said 'What are we gonna do?' So I said 'Leave it to me.' And we were at the back door just standing there in the rain, and Lisa Robinson was there, and all the writers and people who were on the guest list and friends of the band—all the cool people were there, everyone I wanted to be. That's all I wanted, was to be one of the cool people. And everyone went through until it was just me and Merri. And the guy at the rope said 'What do you guys want?' Because we were kids! And I said 'To get out of the rain?' And he let us in. And we said 'Can we stay for the show?' and he said 'Yeah, gahead.' And it became our thing—we kept coming back after that! We were just these two girls by ourselves, and so these ushers sort of took us under their wing and looked out for us. We were like the honorary—like mascots, or pets! And we didn't have to do, you know, sexual— We weren't groupies, we just wanted to see music. And after years of this, we became very brazen and just said 'Hi!' and walked right in."

•

"When Merri and I were listening to Hot Tuna, I had the bright idea, *Let's go to their record company.*"

"What, looking for them?"

"Yes, Michael. That's how naive I was. I thought they'll—"

"They'll just be sitting around. Playing cards, watching *Green Acres*. 'Whatta you guys wanna eat?'"

"Yes, I thought they'll be there, or we can get some pictures and stuff. We never made it past the receptionist, who was astonished. 'Can I help you?' 'We're here for Hot Tuna, please.'"

"'Go right up!'"

"'Well they're not *here*!' Can you imagine?"

"I like the idea they're always together. Like the Fantastic Four."

"I was so dumb. I can't tell you how long before I realized that when you heard a song on the radio, the band wasn't there playing it live."

"No."

"Yes, Michael. I was really dumb."

"But you had records at home. You must've known a DJ was spinning records."

"I believed what I saw on TV. The band was always there together in the studio. I believed everything and everyone. It's a miracle I was never killed. I got into every car, I hitchhiked—and I was always the ringleader. I was always the one who said 'Let's hitchhike to the beach' or 'Let's hitch to King's Plaza.' And we did!"

•

First thing out of school she took a bus to California. This is the seventies. Picture it in Instamatic prints spilling out of a Fotomat envelope. She got off the bus in LA, a guy on a motorcycle followed her along the curb, and she got on.

•

The place was clattering all around us. While she was talking, my eyes were on the grill and its steel backsplash . . . and the steel hood above the griddle . . . and an open flat of eggs . . . and the stacks of plates . . . the white bowls and mugs stacked up—that heavy ceramic . . . and it all had this glow, like we were in the past. After the past few days, everything was illuminated by relief, and gratitude. Isn't the past just the present, minus the uncertainty? Now minus fear.

•

"Why LA?"

"I wanted to go to San Francisco and I thought *Well, I'll stop in LA first.*"

"Why San Francisco?"

"Because of Hot Tuna. That's all I had. I was very angry at my parents for moving to Long Island. My whole life was in Canarsie. All my friends, my music. That's who I was. I was always out of the house: we played stickball in the alley, I played handball by John Wilson 211. I was there every day. Nobody made a plan or a date, they just gathered there. They couldn't get me to come in the house: Mrs. Muttner used to call my mother because she drove by and saw me there smoking pot, smoking cigarettes, and hanging out with a wrong element. And when I was fifteen, they moved to Long Island: completely different universe. People had cars, I didn't. People grew up together and hung out in each other's houses—I didn't know anybody. And I didn't fit in! Everyone was into disco, and I was into—*not* disco. I was of the camp that 'Disco must die!' Y'know? Those T-shirts everyone was wearing. So after three years that I endured going to high school— It was miserable for me. Then my family: 'Go to college, go to college'— begging me to go to college. 'I'm *not* going to college. But I'll tell ya what I *am* doing, I'm *moving* out, and I'm going to California.'"

"[*Laughter*]"

"So I went to the Greyhound bus terminal and I paid seventy-five dollars, and I got my *one-way ticket*—"

"[*Laughter*]"

"Cross-country! On the bus. And they were both aghast: 'What are you gonna do?!' I said, y'know, 'Aah I'll figure it out!'"

●

"What did you think was gonna happen?"

"Adventure. I wanted a whole new thing. All I knew was I wanted to get away from my parents and leave New York and not go to college. I was gonna live in California. There was no— I didn't think it through. There was no *plan*. It wasn't a plan, it was an escape! I didn't do any research, I didn't think you needed a car, I thought it's like New York. It's Los Angeles, it's a big city, I'll walk around. You know, you don't know until you get there. What did I know? I was *so young*—I was too young to live!"

"They must have been terrified. Your daughter's getting on a bus with— I mean, how much money could you have had?"

"I don't know. But I had all the money I ever got. This was like birthday money, Hanukkah money— This was money I saved up. It was money from babysitting or from working as a cashier, when I worked at a market for five minutes . . . I forgot what else I did."

"My first job was dishwasher at a Chinese restaurant."

"That sounds like hard work for a kid."

"Nah."

"I don't know. When I was fifteen, I was a hostess at an IHOP. I didn't have a clue what I was doing. It was my first time walking and talking."

"And you would never think to take a plane, in those days. You were probably never on a plane before."

"The plane never occurred to me. But the *bus* was very appealing, I went and got a knapsack, I thought *Oh*, I bought heavy blue socks: they were very heavy and thick 'cause I thought I might be sleeping outdoors . . . I dunno what I thought, I just was ready for anything."

"Fearless."

"Yes. Brought a notebook, to write everything down . . . and I had an adventure. I got on the bus, I met wonderful people—I met a writer, a poet, gave me one of his books . . . we had a nice long talk . . . uh, I met two boys—younger than me—we got high together . . . I think we did acid? Wound up in Santa Cruz . . . stayed there for a day or so, got back on the bus . . ."

•

"Right away in LA I met this guy at a Fleetwood Mac concert, and I moved in with him."

"Fleetwood Mac?"

"Y'know, I'd go to anything, every show. I met this girl had tickets to Fleetwood Mac. Of all things. And . . . Yeah, I met this guy. I went back with him that night, to Huntington Beach, where he lived."

·

The guy took her out to Colorado and stuck her in a camper.
June paid off his debts with the last of her money. Got a
waitress job at a truck stop.

"I felt very uncomfortable there. We lived with his friends
who had a trailer, and I was helping out with their kids, and
all of a sudden I was in this whole other life that I never
imagined for myself. A woman I worked with was being
abused, and they never saw a Jew before . . . Y'know, I had
this curly hair, they all have accents, believed in Jesus, and
I didn't understand anything about these people or the way
they lived. It was a weird scene. For me to be in—coming
from—y'know, I'm a Jew from Brooklyn! What do I know
about Colorado?"

One of the people she was staying with asked—not
unkindly—to see her horns. Just curious. The next day June
was on a bus to New York.

·

We stepped outside. The rain was done and Second Avenue
was shining—sidewalk, street.

She said "It's all happening too fast!"

I said "But everything that happens happens fast. Right?

However long it takes to happen, when it happens it's an instant."

"But it's only a week! Not even a week. How can we know what this is?"

"When you first hear 'Jumpin' Jack Flash,' how long do you need to know what that is? You know what that is. You know it at the first chord."

•

We wander into St. Mark's Books. Now we're just trying not to say good night. We take things off the shelf, we put them back. It's like you're a teenager and there's nowhere to be, nowhere to land. How do we do this, whatever it is? We walk out of there with a plan to read Proust! Over the phone, if necessary. She wants me take her to the racetrack sometime. You always need some kind of plan, something to go on. I walk her home on dripping side streets.

And then I'm back at my table. Everything different, everything the same.

•

Before dawn, the whine and yawn of garbage trucks below.

•

Philly comes in wearing a beanie, opens his locker, says "Harold, what's gonna be?"

Harold must be 85 years old, he's collapsed on his stool after his workout, barely breathing. Philly's untying his shoes, telling him about his date last night.

He says "I took her to Café Riazor. I get the chicken—you ever had the chicken there?"

With a sad shrug, Harold says "I had the steak, it was wonderful."

"I go for the chicken Riazor. If I was going to the electric chair, you know what I'd have for my last meal? Chicken Riazor. What about you?"

"I don't think I'd have much of an appetite," Harold says, unhappily.

•

Friday morning I'm outside the Y on 14th Street, looking east. She walks right out of the sun. Materializes by the newsstand.

•

Saturday her husband's out of the house from early afternoon till four in the morning, after work. She invited some people over to play cards that night. So I could see Jane and meet a few of her and Jane's friends. Maybe also to keep us from having too much time alone. But by mid-afternoon we've *been* for a walk and *looked* at some old pictures and we're *exhausted* already from lying around on two different pieces of furniture trying to avoid seeing this for what it is, with our words falling out of our mouths because there's nothing more to say and no other way to move forward as she comes over and stretches herself out on their big couch and lays her animal weight on me.

I can say that when June kisses you, you know you've been kissed. You feel like you've been chosen.

In a minute we backed off and got ourselves together. Then we remembered the game. We were jealous of our time alone, which was running out of our veins by the second and pooling on the floor. The prospect of having to pretend in front of other people that there was nothing going on—now that we could no longer pretend it to ourselves—drained me of the will to live. Now we hated that fucking card game. But there it was.

She said "How attached are you to that earring?"

I tossed it out the window.

•

She had a cigar box covered in shiny fabric backstage passes with a stretched-out yellow sparkly hairband around it. And inside, the pale-blue Ticketron stubs from when she first started going to shows at the Garden and the arenas and colleges on Long Island, graduating to the multicolored sunburst design, mostly from the Palladium, MATEUS AT THE PALLADIUM 14TH ST AND 3RD AVE—NO BOTTLES/ CANS—NO REFUNDS/EXCH, some with the venue or date or the name of the act torn off. HOT TUNA WED NOV 24 1976; JORMA KAUKONEN MDNITE SAT NOV 25; ZAPPA DEC 29 1976; November 12, 1976, "Lou Reed" written on the front; "Heart + Jan Hammer + Jeff Beck"; VON LMO 9:00 MON NOV; "Robin Trower + Shooting Star" . . . MOTORHEAD/KROKUS FRI MAY 14 with "David Fricke" written on the back in what appears to be his hand—

David Fricke?

—ELVIS COSTELLO & THE ATTRACTIONS/SQUEEZE JAN 31 1981 . . . plus one with "MOTORHEAD + Ozzy Osborn" in her hand on the front and, on the back, apparently in his hand, "Neil Z 212 769 1148, in Brooklyn." Back when Brooklyn was still 212.

Neil Z?

TUBES MIDNIT SAT APR 28 1979; "Allman Bros."; "English Beat/Pretenders"; GEILS APR 25 1980 . . . CHEAP TRICK MAY 24 1979 . . . MC GUINN/CLARK/HILLMAN FRI APR 13 1979; "Ian Hunter + Mick Ronson" . . . one with

"Student Teachers + Cramps + Iggy Pop" in her hand on the front and, in his on the back: "Bennet Manzella / 2323 Mott Ave / Far Rock. 11691 / 471-3518."

THE RAMONES with "STIV BATORS + the Wanders" written underneath; 10:00P FRI JUL 10; PUBLIC IMAGE LTD 8:00P SUN APR 20 with "James Blood Ulmer/Public Image LTD" on the back of a very soiled stub; THE JAM 8:00P SAT APR 14 1979; THE CLASH FRI MAR 07 1980 with "B Girls/Lee Dorsy" written on the back. THE PATTI SMITH GROUP AUG 10 1979 . . . LEAGUE DEC 07 1977 with "Jerry G." written on the back . . . JOHNNY WINTER 8:00P SUN AUG 07; LITTLE FEAT OCT 5 1978; UTOPIA SUN JUN 20 1976—

Just "Jerry G.," no number.

—BOB DYLAN WED SEP 27 1978; "Grateful Dead" from '79; "Tucker + Outlaws" and "CLAPTON" from '78; NO NUKES CONCERT THUR. SEPT. 20 1979; ZEPPELIN WED. JUNE 8 1977 . . .

Plus the plain little stubs from the Schaefer Music Festival and then the Dr Pepper Music Festival at Wollman Rink, in Central Park: "Joe Jackson" Aug 1 1980; "Peter Tosh" from Sunday, August 19, 1979; JUL 25 "South Side Johnny + the Asbury Jukes" on the front "Larry 471-6437" on the back in his handwriting . . . MONDAY 6:30 P.M. "Stephen Stills"; Central Park Music Festival 14th Year $2.50

"Blondie"; SAT. EVE. 6:30 P.M. JULY 3 "Todd Rundgren/ Cheech + Chong."

Larry? Who the hell is Larry?

Plus, more backstage passes—Jeff Beck, Peter Gabriel, Neon Leon—and tickets from miscellaneous venues: THE STRANGLERS MEN IN BLACK TOUR SATURDAY JUN 20 1981 at Bond; Leon Russell at the Beacon; the Flamin' Groovies at Bottom Line; Jorma at the Capitol Theatre in Passaic; Richie Havens at the Lone Star; David Bromberg at the South Student Center at Nassau Community College; a drink ticket from Club Malibu with "B-52s + Plastics" written on the back; Brother Theodore at 13th Street Repertory; the Undertones at the Diplomat Hotel; the fateful FLEETWOOD MAC 10/2 show at the LA Forum.

At the bottom, there's a broken string of beads, two guitar picks, a Max's pin, some tobacco flakes, and a Marlboro she bummed off of Iggy with a piece of tape around it.

Neil Z? Bennet Manzella from Far fucking Rockaway? Jerry G? Larry, of all people? David fucking Fricke? Iggy fucking Pop?

•

The apartment buzzer goes off, it's Judy Nylon. She comes in with the news that Willy DeVille's got pancreatic cancer.

She just heard he's got two months to live. We talk about Willy DeVille, and then Judy wants to talk writing. She knows from June I'm a writer, and she offers to connect me with someone at *3:AM Magazine*.

"I gave them a segment of my memoir. They're what the *Paris Review* once was. Probably like you, I'm fed up with bullshit dishonest writing no matter how much approval it gets."

"So you're working on a memoir?"

"Off and on, yeah, as I feel it. I struggle with memoir because of the rock thing in my life. I've alway been a sort of samurai in an industry of hardcore gender prejudice and greed, where what you do is either stolen or disregarded and has no history."

"More reason to do it."

"Yeah. Otherwise it's like waiting for someone to ask you to dance."

June's friends BG and Tamar show up, then a guy named Brad. So that's three more people from whom I have to conceal my separation anxiety at losing contact with June. Four, if you count June. And finally, from across the street, Jane, a little bird in black—her usual black tights and a man's black suit jacket with rolled sleeves—immediately the center of any room.

"Jane, it's been a long time. You're looking good."

"Good for what? Look at my hair."

"I gotta hand it to ya."

"I can't believe I left the house like this, I look like Mamie Eisenhower."

She endures a hug and pulls a plastic bag of coins out of her purse.

BG's telling a detailed story about how his nearly pathological persistence with a customer-service employee allowed him to return a pair of slacks he'd been wearing for six months in exchange for a new pair, money back, free hemming, and double air miles. Jane's dealing crazy eights. Judy's talking about reclaiming the rights to her record *Pal Judy.*

"Licensing deal for five years, plus an advance. Then I can buy back the publishing, inshallah."

Then somehow she and Tamar get onto Obama. Brad says "Surely we have more-interesting things than politics to discuss."

"Freddie Herko!" Jane cries.

Laughter all around. "How long you been keeping *that* up your sleeve?" Brad says.

"Who's Freddie Herko?" June wants to know.

"He was a dancer," Brad says. "A Factory person."

"Danced himself out the window onto Cornelia Street," Jane says. She reaches to draw.

"Fifty years ago," Brad says. "Almost."

Jane tells June "I talked to Walter."

"Walter Lure?"

"Yeah."

"He called you?"

"Yeah. He found a photo album with pictures from the eighties."

June, very serious: "How did we look? Did we look fat?"

Jane: "Yeah, especially you."

June: "*Really?*"

Jane: "He said everybody looks good. It was twenty-five years ago: what do you think?"

Later they decide to get a couple of pizzas. So I can breathe, I volunteer to run out and pick them up.

When I get back, Brad's complaining about the new pedestrian plaza in Times Square.

Jane: "Fuckin' Bloomberg. Maybe he can open some more lanes for bicycles to disrupt traffic and run you over."

BG: "While you're having your coffee in the middle of Seventh Avenue. You know, I've gotta say, I've always really wanted to be able to have a coffee there."

Jane: "*How* many *times* have I said 'If only we could have some umbrellas and tables out here!'"

•

To Tere: "Saturday she reminds me she never meant to get involved and she needs her heart back after this marriage.

Then she lies on top of me. Then she says that starting Tuesday, we shouldn't talk for five days while I'm in Cleveland to see my mother. She wants to slow it down. She wants to take it down a notch. But she wants to know what I'm doing today. And tomorrow. Then she says she can't do this, and she doesn't want me to wait. Meanwhile, I can almost see through my hand."

•

The alarm tears me out of sleep by the roots. Black Tuesday. There goes Manhattan, behind corrugated barriers on the BQE. Town Car to LaGuardia: bad shocks and greasy seats and pink deodorizer. "It's good you're going away," she said. "Let's agree to not talk while you're gone." The radio's tuned to an R&B station. We shoot the rapids near Broadway/37th Street, Queens. They've been working on this stretch of road for thirty years. "No, don't write. I have to list my house, get divorced, find a new place, plus keep up with my job." The driver's geared up for the court in a jersey, long silky shorts, giant shoes. "I feel like I've been on vacation and now I have to pay attention to my life. And I can't do that if I'm talking to you." Sun flaring in the grass. Purple cornflower, Queen Anne's lace.

•

In Cleveland, I wasn't much company for anyone. Five days no contact. The only thing worse than being alone was being with people. When someone was speaking to me I felt like my soul was being dragged through a small hole at the base of my skull. Was she backing out? Hoping the train would slow down so she could jump off? I watched TV with my mother. I took her to the store with my aunt and fixed dinner for them. At night I got in the car and drove around, listening to music and smoking cigarettes.

•

To Tere: "You say if it's meant to be, it'll be. Meant by whom? God? Cupid? I know *I* wasn't looking for this. I was happy to spend the next thirty or forty years catching up on my reading. For two years I never shut up about how grateful I was to be alone. Then someone leaves the gate open and I'm out of it like a shot. Maybe that's why I feel so desperate. I'm out of control."

•

When my mother went to bed I sat on the apartment balcony, smoking, watching the night above the trees, sorting back through every conversation with June until I came across something I could pin my hopes on. Now and then a car went past. Down below, a skunk left the shadows and came into the parking lot.

•

"Obviously she's got a lot going on. Emotionally, psychologically, logistically. And she's still living with her husband until they sell their apartment. But experience tells me there's no such thing as a clean slate, and at some point life kicks your door open. Old people understand this, they don't have all these notions about when things should and shouldn't happen. They know life is short, and things happen when they happen. Grab a shirt and go."

•

I got out of the car at the supermarket. The entrance was a hundred yards away. With each step I sank into the asphalt like it was rubber. So I just stood there.

Slow time down enough and it hurts to be alive.

I wasn't sure I could make it across the lot. People were pushing carts, loading their trunks. Why do so many people out here dress like toddlers?

I pressed on.

Because the alternative was what? Just let my life unwind in a parking lot outside of Heinen's?

•

After dinner I was getting on the freeway and at the top of the ramp a big pink cloud was piled on the sky. And I saw that nothing was wrong, everything was okay.

How many times had a late advent of sunlight opened something inside me? A perspective. Always in response to stress or dread. That's the only time I could ever master time's trick, and only for a moment. I remember a Sunday before the first day of school, 7:30 in the evening: I'm looking out the apartment window as the sun melts in a tangle of black branches. I could only have been seven or eight, but the moment lives on . . .

Happiness is just a change in the light.

•

Next morning I paced the balcony like a crackhead in a holding cell. Waiting to fly home for her decision. As crazed at 50 as I was at 15.

The last time I was on that balcony with my old man, I was waiting to go to the airport. Hot afternoon. We were sitting in silence, I was gazing into the heat. He appeared to be dozing.

Then, without opening his eyes, he said "This afternoon,

I'm going to consider . . . the categorical imperative . . . of Immanuel Kant."

I looked at him.

"Try to figure out what he was driving at," he said.

I laughed.

He said "I was fascinated by these guys. All the time I spent reading about them in college, and all I remember is that Kant took a walk every day, Spinoza ate dried apricots, and Schopenhauer played the flute."

•

I call her as soon as I land. I don't even wait to get in a cab, I'm still in the line. No answer. Right away I start to panic. Even though I know her husband's off Sundays. By the time I get back home my hands are cold.

South 2nd Street is quiet. Couple of guys playing dominoes outside the bodega.

Then she calls. Asks about my flight as though nothing's changed. As though everything's normal. As though I'm not this insane speeding monkey over here. She'll have a couple of hours after today's open house . . .

•

Sammy scratched on a transom window of the J

•

Back home, I put on my reading glasses and I can see the weave of my jeans and the sunlit dust particles on the midnight-blue cover of my writing tablet, and there's a flooding, swimming sensation at the world as it is and my ability to apprehend it. Bars of sunlight on the couch. They brighten and fade with the breeze. They come back, and fade. Everybody's coming out after the rain, banging pots and pans, blowing plastic horns. The sky's in the puddles, and people come out from the bodega awnings and door-ways, out of the alleys, and with singing, with cymbals and timbrels and psalteries and harps, with trumpets, and up from the sewers and out of the parks, bringing gold, and silver, ivory, and apes, and peacocks. And with conchs and kettledrums, tabors and cowhorns. And snatching laundry off the lines, flying it like flags. "Come on, come on, come on!" Oh, my baby . . .

Standing on the corner, gym bag in my hand. Here comes Lou, on his way out already at seven a.m.

"What's the action?" he says.

"You're done?"

"Yeah, I was here five o'clock. Now I'm running all day. The Judge is peddling a script, he asked if I get it to De Niro. I'll leave it at the office in Tribeca, with a note."

I see the Judge in the morning two rows over. Tough customer, carries himself like an ex-champ: everything just so. I always seem to catch him in the mirror in his shorts, fixing his tie, with a shirt straight out of plastic—always a blue shirt with a white collar. A New York Supreme Court judge, but he wrote a couple of crime novels, and they made movies out of them.

One time my pal Phil Dray had jury duty with the Judge presiding. During jury selection, they asked Phil what he does for a living. At that point, Phil had a new book about the Mississippi Burning murders. The Judge interrupts, he wants a word. "Can the juror approach the bench?" The lawyers are looking at each other—"What's this now?" Phil goes up. The Judge leans down—"Tell me: who was your agent on that book?"

Lou says "I'm not in touch with these guys lately, I ain't had much action since *Analyze That*. But I'll take the script downtown. The Judge was up to Rao's—he hangs out with Sonny Grosso—but he couldn't get nowhere with it."

Sonny Grosso's one of the cops who made the French Connection bust. Done some cameos, some producing. Same as Frank Pellegrino, the owner of Rao's. While Lou's talking I get a glimpse of this world of producers and actors and mob guys and cops and judges, and they're all the same people, and all anyone cares about is the movies. A little action.

•

And then I'm leaning on the wall outside the Y, reading a book. Later, June says about this time, "It's like I was young again. The anticipation! Every day was a gift. And I knew you were going to be there, even the first time. God, that was exciting! Can't explain it. That was very exciting."

•

To Tere: "Today she was out walking around for lunch and she called. I told her I'd walk up the east side of Broadway.

I spotted her coming down the west side, looking a little disoriented. I couldn't imagine going around as that person. With all those curls, there was something improbable about her, bold and oblivious, different from the rest of us. She was like a mythical creature. Who found her way onto Broadway. I don't recall ever feeling so happy. Just to *see* someone. Same thing yesterday, when she asked me to meet her after work, and I sat on my couch all afternoon, waiting, needing nothing more. And since there was no danger of sex, I knew it was just about her."

•

We get an hour and a half before work. All the time in the world. We ride the 1 to Columbus Circle. Walk to a diner. She gets oatmeal and I get eggs. Settle up, I walk her back to One Time Warner, and our time is up. It always seems like a great wealth of time divided into shorter and shorter segments that expand as they get fewer until, always too soon, I'm watching her walk to the escalator, across the soaring atrium. I watch her all the way there, and she turns and waves. Up the escalator, she waves again—

And then I'm through the glass to the sky's-the-limit that's waiting for me, and I'm moving down Eighth Avenue— lucky in the world—through Midtown's multiverse of intersecting reflections in the fresh morning roar.

•

jackhammers

•

We tipped the couch over backward, wound up on the floor with me on top of her. She had on white lace panties, I could see her bush. I got her jeans halfway down and remembered I didn't have anything with me.

"You suck!" she said.

•

Five a.m., thunder in the dark: two long, soft, satisfying, reticulated unrollings of it, and then—complete rain. I lie there listening. There's a flash of lightning through my eyelids, and then another soft, long roll of thunder, like a bolt of carpet bouncing down heaven's stairs. Somehow, the rain increases. For a moment, I can hear the shapes of things in the rain like a blind man. A nearer crack of thunder starts three car alarms—two on this block. The rain increases again and there's a war whoop from the street, then mad laughter, then "Yo! I'll tell you about that tomorrow!" By 5:14 it's over and the room has lightened, a few silver rainbeads

hanging from the open sill, a cool breeze turning the blades
of the window fan.

·

There's that moment after you open your eyes, just a few seconds before you put the world back together, before you're
anyone in particular. You're looking at a slice of light between the window frame and the shade. Then you take up
your identity, with its memories and preconceptions, and it's
the same day as yesterday. But now I remember June. I wake
up in my old life and then I remember I'm in a new life.
And lie there listening to the birds and the BQE. Morning
docked at the window like an ocean liner.

·

Then guess what? Her husband went to Thailand for a week.
I guess he booked it when she asked for a divorce. Before
they listed their place, she hired a painter to touch it up and
took a few days off. I couldn't believe my luck.

We were on top of the sheets in Brooklyn, in the afternoon. Window wide open behind the shade. It was after, I
was lying on my arm, taking her in. She caught me looking
and pulled back.

She said "You look like you're gonna cry!"

I cracked up.

●

Over under sideways down. Days of fucking, the window-shade now lofted on a breeze, now tapping at the frame, clothes on the floor, lips puffy from kissing, jaw sore, tongue sore, raw below, eyes drowsy with beyond. Days out of time. Reawakened to your animal self, which lives to fuck and fucks to live, or dies, and everything else is bullshit.

●

Kevin and Philly are getting dressed, talking between two rows of lockers about doo-wop. Philly says he used to sing on the street, growing up in Brooklyn. Lou comes in to give me something from the paper and I grab his magazines from my locker. He's wearing gigantic full-protection sunglasses over his regular glasses, as though he's been to an eye appointment. With an irritated wave of the hand, he dismisses the doo-wop era as a childish excitement. He can let nothing Kevin says go unchallenged, for it's each man's role to disagree with the other about everything.

Talking to me across their conversation, he says "I never cared for it, doo-wop."

"No? Not even looking back?"

"I rejected the whole thing," he says. "I never liked the staccato singing. That staccato line. I prefer *legato*, the long line."

He demonstrates the difference by singing a verse of some old sentimental song in both styles, first keeping time with a strict karate-chop gesture, and then crooning sweetly to me among the lockers and half-naked men, eyebrows raised, conducting a long, fluid line. Meanwhile, Kevin and Philly are talking about Ruby and the Romantics.

Pointing back and forth between us, Lou says "This is like you and me talking about Burger King."

"What's this now?" Kevin says. "What're you saying, Lou?"

"Like hamburgers," Lou says. "This is like you wanna talk about hamburgers, but instead of talking about P.J. Clarke's, you're talking about Burger King." He pulls a frown and shrugs.

"You're a thug, Lou. You don't know what you're—"

"In the upper echelons of music, these people are never spoken of," Lou tells Philly, who's pulling on a pair of red pants and trying to stay out of it. "These people are not in the pantheon."

Kevin says "If it's not Jimmy Roselli or Jerry Vale, you're not interested."

Lou turns to him, explaining as though to a child. "This

is like you want veal Parmesan, but you're going to the Olive Garden instead of Il Mulino."

"Nobody cares about those guys," Kevin says. "Jimmy Roselli's for the birds."

"Oh!"

"Aoh!"

"Oh, now you said it!" Philly says.

"Don't *ever*—" Lou begins.

"If his name was Roseliwitz, you wouldn't give a shit about him."

Lou pantomimes astonishment. "Don't *ever* let people hear you say that," he cautions. "Don't ever let people who know about music hear you say that. You know why? Because when you leave, they're gonna say"—and here he rolls his eyes and slowly shakes a limp hand—"Ma-*don'*, this guy— Did you hear what he said? This guy's *ubazz'*!"

"Aah, Louie," Philly says. "Nothing's been the same since Perry Como died."

•

I was looking past her curls at the building across the street—we were both facing south. She dropped her head and clenched one fist.

•

To Tere: "She's excited by things I'm jaded about. Walking around Williamsburg. Sitting in the dark in a place like a shop that outfits whaling ships, eating a cut of meat you first heard of two weeks ago that's on every menu now. Or going to any of these other New Brooklyn places that take authenticity to a spurious extreme. But it's new to her, so it's fun.

"At Aqueduct I have to use the restroom, so I leave her on a vacant bench, in a half-lit corner, near a closed concession. When I come back, she's between twelve guys asking who she likes in the early double.

"She doesn't want to bet, she just wants to see the place. Wants to know if we can pet the horses. Just before post time I talk her into splitting a three-horse exacta box: 2/4/5. We're at the finish line when they run past just like that. With the 3 out front. She's already flipping through the program—'Can we bet another one?'"

•

Summer breakfast: an iced coffee and a nectarine.

•

Lou's coming toward me on 14th Street in the sun.

He says "Where you going?"

"I'm going the gym, I'm late today. You got your summer cut? Looks good."

He says "My six-month haircut. January first, July first. He charges me seventeen dollars. I give him twenty-five. Fifty a year. A dollar a week."

"Very good, Lou."

"Aright: Mike! Let me go," he says, as though I've detained him long enough.

•

"Everything's a first. Shopping for dinner, running a handful of blackberries under the faucet while fixing breakfast. Waking up at grey dawn to coolness in the sheets and warmth where skin creases and a whiff of sweat and dried sex in a tenement room with thirty coats of white paint on the walls. Really, with her, just doing laundry would be a thrill."

•

She's making the bed in an A-shirt and boxers, hair up.

•

To Tere: "This week is deliriously good. Her husband's away, we're together every minute we can be. But I'm living in the shadow of the future. She keeps saying 'This is a gift. This week is a gift.' Which I hear as 'This will never happen again.' When I get near the subject of the future, she says 'I don't know what that looks like.'

"She's keeping a spreadsheet of things we should do. Including countries to visit. But she doesn't know what's going to happen and doesn't want me to wait. Meanwhile she wants a shelf for all her stuff in my bathroom."

•

I started to say it—we were in bed—she saw it in my eyes—I was saying it—"I—"

"Don't say it!" she said.

•

"Kevin, what's that carrot salad recipe with the pepper flakes?"

He looms over me with a towel around his waist—he's a big dude. "Two pounds of carrots, cut on the bias, and then cut each piece in three. Bigger than a matchstick. Throw 'em in boiling water for three minutes—"

"Salted water?"

"Very salty water, three minutes, till they're just a little—"

"Yeah."

"Then *immediately* toss them in a bowl with six table-spoons of red-wine vinegar, dried oregano, four cloves of garlic *sliced thick* so you can find them. Because they turn blue in the vinegar."

"Okay."

"And four bay leaves, you toss it all up. Salt and pepper, of course. And then just enough olive oil to make it shine. And leave it sit for twenty-four hours. And every time you walk past, you give it a stir."

"It's in the fridge or out?"

"Out. And always stirring. And that goes good with anything—with meat, whatever."

"Yeah, same as all these cold salads with oil and vinegar. Tuna with onion, lentil salad, I make. Beet. Cucumber with dill. Even chopped cabbage with oil and vinegar."

"I take a wedge of cabbage and a head of radicchio, couple of radishes, a few cherry tomatoes, and then salami cut into little rods, toss that with oil and vinegar, it's delicious."

"Wait, what's that last one again?" A voice from down the aisle. Kevin starts it again.

"Wait, wait—" The guy goes into his gym bag for a notebook. "I'm going to a picnic tomorrow . . ."

•

The window gate's swung open, the window's open wide. She's got her head on my chest and I'm looking past the fire escape at Sunday morning. Yesterday we stopped at a Dominican place under the J tracks and got a *morir soñando.* "To die dreaming." Today her husband gets back. If I were dying, the building across the street would be the most beautiful one I ever saw. Not the Duomo, not Fallingwater, not the Flatiron. Just a yellowbrick tenement in the sun on South 2nd Street.

•

One of the signs of summer: a molten trickle down the outside of the Vermeer. Orange, mute. Every summer I watch it from the pillow. After June found a buyer, she spent eight months on Jane's couch and then bought a studio here, right across the street. Fourteenth and Seventh. What's this, our third summer here? I can't keep track. July's July. Every July is all Julys. I sort my memories by the month. By the season. Don't we all? The studio looks north, to the Chrysler Building and the Empire State. From the sleeping alcove we see an outside wall at a right angle to us. Early in the morning, the water that's dripped down the wall from an air conditioner mirrors the eastern sky.

•

Every morning I was outside the Y on 14th Street, waiting for June. Life doesn't get better. That expectant point is as good as life gets. I was watching the world and myself in it. On the point of the present moment with room to move around in it. Waiting is what I was made of. And I trusted she would show. And I couldn't believe I trusted it but I was starting to. We were like a rubber raft: maybe it's wobbly climbing on, but that thing's not going down.

She disappears in the sun with the people crossing Sixth Avenue and reappears by the newsstand. And when she does, I've already spotted her. Something in me sees her before I do. It's gnosis! Before the sight of her has made its way through the bureaucracy of my cognition, I'm on it. There's a hole that only she fills. She coincides perfectly with the possibility of June.

I watch her come. We're trying not to smile, but she hits me with it because who cares, and then we're wrapped in the heat of those smiles and waiting is overtaken by experience.

•

"Rao's expensive, Lou?"

"Nah, not really. Hundred a head. And they give you a lot of food. I know the guy. Frankie Pellegrino. They call him Frankie No. Cuz all he says is no. All day long, people call up: 'Frankie, can I get a table?' 'No.' 'Frankie, you got—' 'No.' The place is a gold mine. It's tiny. Six booths and four tables. And only one seating per night."

"It's good?"

"It's alright. It's okay. He invited me up there one time, I said 'Frank. First of all it's too far. I gotta go to 114th Street? Second, it's too late. I'm in bed seven, eight o'clock. And Frank. Most important, I cook better food than you."

I laughed.

He said "I used to get invited there every Thursday night by Tony Dime, he was a wiseguy, but he died now. You gotta have your own table there or get invited by someone who does. Woody Allen's got a table, Sonny Grosso . . ."

"How's that work? Obviously Woody Allen doesn't go there every night."

"No, Mondays, his table. He's not coming he calls up: 'Frankie, I can't make it.' Then either he sends someone else or they give the table away that night."

"I see."

"I went there once in the day."

"They're open for lunch?"

"No, they're cleaning up. I had to go to 116th Street, see a guy, and it was a hot day, I needed some water. I was parched. So I tapped on the door, they opened up. Two guys were there sweeping up. I said 'I need a glass of water, I'm dying.' They said 'Come on in.' I didn't tell Frankie about it, he'd say 'What're these guys doing, letting people in?' They took me to the bar, the guy said 'I'm gonna give you some water from Nicky Vest's private stock of mineral water.'"

"Who's that?"

"Nicky Vest? The bartender, he's been the bartender there fifty years. Always wears a vest."

•

The sycamore near the corner of South 2nd and Marcy rustles with my childhood secrets. Secret even from me. Some things, when you notice them, turn out to have been ongoing. That alarm bell started behind the shopping center, when I was a kid in Ohio.

•

I was riding in a Town Car with Jane to Home Depot, my Friday off. Before Jane fired her driver. She was tough, but after a year or two she got past her doubts about me. A Stevie Wonder song came on the radio. She was looking out the window, moving her head.

"You ever work with Stevie Wonder?"

". . . Yeah," she said. Her mind was elsewhere.

"When was that?"

"I did his press from 1971 to 1978 or '9."

"Those were great years for him, no?"

Madison Square Park was going by.

She said "He used to play at eleven in the morning. You know, like a Motown revue? And they were the *best* shows."

"I bet. But he wasn't still doing those shows when you had him, right?"

She said "I took the Faces to see Stevie there, it was the best day of their lives."

"You took the *Faces* to see Stevie Wonder?"

"At the Apollo, yeah. They couldn't believe it. They were such cute little guys. Like little elves. They always came to see me after that. Whenever one of 'em was in town. Ian, the two Ronnies . . . so sweet . . ."

Eventually I found out there was no one in the music business she hadn't worked with or crossed paths with.

Once I said "What about Sly Stone? You ever have anything to do with him?"

"No," she said.

"Really?"

"No. Well. I did his wedding. At Madison Square Garden."

At Home Depot we made our way up and down. After a while it was hard to tell if we were shopping or just hanging out there.

"What's with your knee?" I asked her. "Why are you walking like that?"

"I don't wanna talk about it."

"Is your knee bothering you?"

"Maybe a little. Only when you annoy me, but I'm not blaming you."

•

flatbed truck double-parked with a delivery of scaffold

•

Lou's getting dressed and Philly comes in, they're at neighboring lockers. I ask Lou what he's doing today, he says running errands. I tell him we're going to Park Slope to see friends.

"That whole neighborhood," Lou says. "It's all a historic district now. All protected. Even more than the Village."

"Park Slope, baby," Philly says. "That's where I grew up."

"No. Really?"

He's wearing an off-white guayabera and loose linen slacks, hair slicked back. He looks great.

"I grew up right near there. Sunset Park. Where Albert Anastasia shot Arnold Schuster."

"Who's Arnold Schuster?"

"The guy who ratted out Willie Sutton."

"Shoe salesman," Lou says, with derision that borders on pity.

"What, Anastasia was offended? Willie Sutton wasn't a mob guy, right? I thought he was a bank robber."

"That's right," Philly says. "Willie Sutton was a wanted man. Arnold Schuster spotted him on the subway. He got off the train and called the cops."

"They interviewed Schuster on TV," Lou says. "Anastasia was home in his easy chair."

"Anastasia saw him on TV and picked up the phone. They put six bullets in him."

"'Cause he was a rat," Lou says, getting his shopping bag in order. He carries a big plastic Duane Reade handle bag wherever he goes. "Principle of the thing."

•

Saturday morning after the farmers' market we came back to the Vermeer and she spent the day around the apartment, no makeup, in a baby-blue *Metallic KO* T-shirt.

She's had it forever. She wore it the first Saturday we met up there, and it was old then.

In those first months, we met in the city after work. Holding hands on the darker side streets, pushing into doorways, releasing each other at the subway.

Fridays I was off. I dusted, swept, and mopped the apartment. All in happy anticipation. Then maybe I walked down to Tops, on North 6th, to shop for dinner. Dropped it home. Walked to the other side of the BQE and bought a loaf of semolina bread. Stopped at Fortunato's for biscotti and carried them back in a white box tied with string. No rush. Got dinner started. Beef stew with a salad of escarole and endive. Or cod stew with tomatoes and fennel and green olives. Lima beans in tomato sauce with celery and potatoes. Once I made rice pudding for dessert. I spent all day getting ready. Then I walked to meet her at the subway feeling enlivened and calm.

Saturdays it was Union Square, as soon as she could get away. We walked through the market for what looked good and then got the train straight back to Brooklyn. Because she could never spend the night, we were always on the meter.

Her bag open on my couch with its already-bent copy of *Lunch Poems* jammed in there. Her panties on the floor, and the sheets mostly too. Midnight we walked to the subway.

Then I walked back. Under the BQE, trucks blasting overhead, past the locked playground. Up Marcy. Sundays he was home, they showed the apartment. So tomorrow nothing. I'd let myself into the building. Toss the watermelon rinds and go to bed.

•

I'm seeing this as a plein air novel. Written on the fly. Since I quit smoking, a few months after we got together, I'm averse to writing routines. So I write when I feel like it. Sitting on a standpipe. On the train. At the gym. Which is where I am now: downstairs at the Y, across from the pool, watching a swimmer on the other side of the glass. I used to wait here on Sundays so June and I could steal an hour when she got done showing her place. I started carrying a notebook so we wouldn't lose a moment, since any moment, together or apart, was one of ours. "I sit here watching, blank and alive, like a cat. The lights on the pool, a swimmer's arm, a splash: all you."

•

So you walked out of the bus station in LA and got on the *first bike that rolled up*? Have I got that right?

•

Once, walking home from Elinor and Maggie's roof party, we stopped at B&H. A woman down the counter had her wrist in a cast.

June said "I always wanted a cast. I never had a cast, braces—none of the things everybody else had in my neighborhood. I wished I could break my collarbone so I could have one of those cool neck braces. I had a little brother, that was it. Couldn't have a dog, I wasn't allowed. Not even an invisible dog."

"How could they stop you from having an invisible dog?"

"Do you know about this? How do you know about this?"

"An invisible dog?"

"We went to a carnival with the Kolodnys, you could get like a—"

"It was a leash."

"Yes! I thought *This is the perfect thing! I'm not allowed to have a dog in the house—this is the perfect solution.* I wanted it so bad. 'She doesn't need it.' Gary Kolodny told my father 'Let her have it! What's the matter with you? It's not a real dog!' 'No.'"

We sat there without saying anything. They brought our order. I had a tuna melt and a chocolate egg cream, June had a classy discreet cold borscht. I was picturing her as a kid.

"Did you have a bike?"

"Of course I had a bike, I was everywhere on my bike. Used to go around the block to get a slice . . . Carvel . . . Used to play ringolevio . . ."

"What is ringolevio, exactly?"

"It's like hide-and-seek but more sophisticated."

"How's it more sophisticated?"

"There's a song."

•

Sometimes I wake up thinking what's outside the window is what was outside my bedroom window where I grew up, with the sound of far-off lawn mowers moving among the apartment lawns and the other sounds of a summer morning. Today there were voices from the street, one guy blaming another for showing up two hours late last night on dope. I wouldn't have heard that from my room in Ohio. But it took time and reasoning to believe there was something out there other than the view from that boy's room.

•

Hot Brooklyn morning I walk to the subway behind two kids who're so into each other they can hardly walk straight. They're just sort of knocking down the street. The universe collapses for a second when a dump truck bounces over a metal plate, but do they notice? Nah, they're inside it like you're inside a hangover. I recognize it right away, it's coming off of them like fumes in the heat . . .

•

"Okay, Tere, it happened. The package from AARP. Of course I've been getting spam for Cialis for years. And lately it's been Silver Singles, hip replacements, reverse mortgages, funeral plots, and those electric carts people in the rest of the country buzz around on with a bag of Doritos and a little American flag. But yesterday I got the big envelope by U.S. mail, welcoming me to old age. AARP card and application, letter of introduction, decals, a bumper sticker, sample issue of the magazine, return-address labels, cardboard visor, the whole bit.

"Then I go to see Philly's band at a bar in the Village. As his alter ego Ollie Boy Lester, Philly fronts a jazz band, and some of the guys from the Y go to show their support. I'm at the bar with him before the set, he says 'Do you know Patsy?'—another guy from the locker room. Patsy says to me 'You grew up with him in Brooklyn?' Now, Philly's sixty-four. I ain't even fifty. Maybe to Patsy, who's frail, jaundiced, and disappearing down the tunnel of the years, it's all the same.

"Later, Lou puts him in a cab. It's a struggle, Patsy's trembling, one of the new cabs you have to climb up. Lou gives him a hand.

"Cab pulls away, Lou says under his breath '*La vecchiaia è brutta. La vecchiaia è carogna.*'

"Translation: Old age is ugly. Old age is carrion."

•

"Tell me again what a burrito is?" she says.

How's that for Brooklyn attitude?

I start to describe it, but she's already decided it's not for her and stopped listening.

"I can't believe you never had a burrito. Even by accident. On the road. From a gas station or something."

There's a pause as she's scanning the menu card.

"What else?" she says, distracted.

"What else what?"

"What else?" As in *What else is on your mind?*

•

SHAFTWAY

•

So there was Neil Z and Bennet and Jerry and Larry, got it, and possibly David Fricke, okay. Anyone else on the *Rolling Stone* staff? Other periodicals? Okay. Just let me— Frank Zappa's *microphone tech*, was it?

•

I take Lou his magazines and wind up sitting on the couch with him for half an hour while he waits for Father Joe. I tell him I spent six fish yesterday on a pint of fresh figs, he says he turned down the strawberries at Union Square because they were $12 a quart. I tell him I have a friend in San Francisco who goes two days a week without food and cite the ancient Egyptian proverb that says a quarter of what you eat feeds you and the other three quarters feeds your doctor. Further,

I point him to a theory that fasting allows the liver to stop producing a growth hormone that causes cancer. Lou tells me about the calf's liver at Le Zie, *à la Venezia*. I tell him I don't eat liver and he asks what about *vestedda* (spleen)? As if to illustrate our discussion, a man appears at the top of the stairs in a summer-weight cap and short-sleeve shirt, with a belt cinched around a pair of suitpants of about the same vintage as the Marshall Plan. "Here's a V-man," Lou says. He points out anyone who lives at the Vermeer: "Another V-man," he'll say. "This guy's a V-man." He introduces me to Gene, the man in the cap. Gene says he's 96 years old, never sick a day in his life, last time he's in a hospital was in North Africa, in 1944, with appendix. Lou asks him about his appetite. Gene says "I don't eat much. But I never did." Lou and I exchange a meaningful nod. Then Father Joe comes in, another bird-light nonagenarian, all smiles, radiating goodwill and a clear conscience, and Lou gives him a Danish and today's papers, and Lou and I walk down the street. He tells me he's going home to make himself, though he knows he shouldn't, a soppressata sandwich, because he's got the soppressat' in the fridge and it shouldn't go to waste, and anyway who can resist?

•

I grabbed a handful of curls. The window shade dragged against the wall. When I came it tore out of me like something barbed—something I didn't know was even there.

After dinner we went again. Then I stretched out beside her and sank my face in her hair.

She said "Oh my God. You're my revenge. Against everything."

"I feel like a chopped-down tree."

•

We walked out of the Giglio Festival and under the BQE with a bag of zeppole. *I* had the zeppole, who'm I kidding? Behind us, the lights on the rides were blinking in the dusk.

She said "I hate that ride, that gravity-defying ride."

"I give 'em all a wide berth. What rides do you like?"

"I like the Cyclone."

"Doesn't surprise me that you like roller coasters."

"That's what I like, Mike: I like punk music and roller coasters."

•

Sometimes when we got separated in a public place—we're in a store, I don't see her—I had a moment of *How'd I get here?* Like maybe I was waking up, and there was no June after all.

I found Lou on the stair machine, climbing nowhere, with the *Daily News* over the monitor and the other papers in a stack on the floor behind him. I put five copies of *Fortune* on the stack.

"Lou, we went to a wedding this weekend I met a guy eats nothing but raw food."

"Supposed to be very good for you," he said. "There's a whole movement now."

"This guy cured himself of diabetes. And Lyme disease."

"I believe it."

"But where do you get protein?" I said. "You can't eat raw beans."

"Tofu?" he said. "Is that cooked?"

"I dunno."

He thought about it.

"Prosciut' isn't cooked," he said. "They cure it. You could eat that."

"That's right. All the prosciut' and capocol' you can eat. You're onto something, Lou."

•

After dinner I walked to Graham Avenue for an ice. I walked back on Conselyea, as the leaves darkened and the color drained out of the sky. A GTO convertible was parked at the curb with the top down. And there between day and night I heard the wind in the trees, and felt it moving out of my past, through my life, on my face.

•

slithery seams of tar in the street

•

We wake up at the Vermeer on top of the sheets with the windows open wide. Same temperature as last night.

She says "I feel like I was drugged."

"It's like you're dragged back into the same day."

"That's exactly right."

"Like you slept on the sidewalk."

"Are you ready for coffee?"

"Or the hood of a car."

She's on her way to the kitchen.

"June—"

"Bun."

"Like a migrant worker who slept in a ditch."

"Do you want hot coffee, or iced?"

•

the smell of a dead mouse in the weeds in the morning

•

She said "I'd like to get even closer to you, but I can't."

"I know. If it were up to me, we'd sift together like sand, until we were inseparable."

•

Seven a.m. and the day already smells like something that's been in a dumpster overnight.

•

She got off the bus in LA, a guy on a motorcycle rolled up beside her, and she got on.

•

In the subway between Sixth and Seventh, the guy selling incense has got the whole tunnel choked with nag champa: "Take a look take a look take a look!" Upstairs, the sky gets darker and darker, almost black. And then the rain comes down in a white hissing torrent, the little rooftop trees are bent with it, but behind the rain, the sky has already lightened.

•

Humid air blowing up the subway stairs smells like the pachyderm house at the zoo.

•

Walked you to the subway, went home and waited for your call.

Now it's just me in here, with a notebook.

But writing to myself seems like a step in the wrong direction. Toward myself, away from us.

Something happened in there tonight. Right? Something more. Like now there was nothing below us. Or there was more to it than just you and me on a bed.

•

Saturday morning the guys are getting dressed, they're talking about music. Manny recalls the Flamingos' "I Only Have Eyes for You."

"Written by Harry Warren," Lou says. He stayed out of it until credit was due to an Italian. "Born Salvatore Guaragna, 1893. From Coney Island."

Philly says "I remember the first time I heard it! You remember those trucks they used to park in the street with the rides, for the kids? It was playing on one of the rides. This was 1958, '59—Mikey wasn't even born yet. I saw the Flamingos at one of the Alan Freed shows."

Saul, who's tall and glum and usually silent, speaks up from the next row. His voice comes over the lockers. "The Christmas Jubilee? With Jackie Wilson?"

Philly goes to the end of the row to answer him. "I saw the Flamingos at the Easter Jubilee at the Brooklyn Paramount." He comes back saying "But I saw Jackie Wilson at the Brooklyn Fox. Man, he was so great—he had that song 'You Better Know It.' He was better than anybody."

"Mr. Perpetual Motion," Lou supplies.

"No, Mr. Excitement."

Saul, over the lockers: "At the Labor Day show? I was there."

Philly says "It was Chuck Berry, the Everly Brothers, the Elegants had 'Little Star'—"

Saul: "Bo Diddley!"

"Four in the morning, I met the guys on the block and we walked there. Thirteen years old. And we stood on line till they opened the doors at nine forty-five."

I said "You and Saul were on the same line."

"I *saw* Saul! He was only this big, then."

"That's right," comes the voice. "We argued about Eisenhower. Philly was just about to vote for Nixon."

"That's right!" Philly says. "And Saul was a Commie even then."

•

Saturday afternoon at the Vermeer, reading on the bed. I keep looking up from the book to the outside wall, with its window reflecting water towers and rooftops and sky. A view like an old linen postcard. Read another page or two. Back to that window, and those cutouts climbing against the sky in jumbled reds, blonds, and browns, doubled in the glass, no weight, no mass, no movement. Pigeons.

•

Before she left here last night, she sat on my leg at the table and I took a picture of us with her phone. Today she sent it. And although she was here two nights till midnight, and yesterday we were together all day, the picture's a surprise, like a photo from when you were young. That transcendent glow. The way she's looking at me. That she'd want a picture. That she'd send it. Sometimes, it seems improbable that she should say my name. I guess you spend so much time thinking about something, you're startled when there's evidence of it in the world.

·

One morning I was reading in bed, June was still asleep.

"Hear the birds?" I said.

Pretty soon there was a little smile on her face. It was the incipient smile of figures in religious paintings and children's drawings.

She had a feeling for birds. We'd wake up in the morning and she'd say "Ohh. Do you hear him? He's back." The sound made her aware of another dimension. Like opening a window, or stepping outside. Unlocked the wider world, or a more complex worldview. One that included nature in the city.

That *ohh* was something that just escaped her. As if she remembered something she forgot to do, or a life she forgot to lead.

A few days before, in the subway, I saw a white bar of sunlight on the wall, shot in from above. You know, it's only there at a certain time of day. It's there on the wall, this unremarked fact.

Sitting up in bed, I thought maybe the birds were for her what that patch of sunlight was for me. Information from elsewhere, like the breeze.

·

Back in our second month, I'm telling Tere: "So far I've dropped fifteen pounds. Back to my fighting weight of one thirty. For burning calories, there's nothing like romantic distress. Round-the-clock mental activity. Better than cardio. She keeps saying 'I don't know what's going to happen.' Imagine hearing that from your lawyer. Or surgeon. Consumed as I am with her past and our future—anything but *right now*—I'm a furnace of mental activity."

•

She has an event tonight, so for lunch we meet halfway at a diner on Seventh Ave. Omelette for her, sardines on rye for me. Greek place with Spanish staff. LA PARISIENNE RESTAURANT / STEAKS CHOPS & SEAFOOD / EST. 1950

•

On a warm afternoon an overcast sky in the shine on the floor . . .

•

Across from me on the L, two girls were trading a nod. Doing the statue. You don't see it much anymore. One of them was holding her hands rigid as though she got her nails done last night and forgot to relax. The other—wearing a huge white flower in her hair like a dahlia that fluttered slightly as though with the speed of the train, as though she were in timelapse—was trying to drink a Pepsi but too busy dreaming to get the bottle to her mouth or tilt it sufficiently when she did. Eyes closed, she lifted it to her cheek for a minute or two, and then got it to her mouth and kept it there for about three stops, the Pepsi sloshing around in the bottom of the bottle, until her face creased in irritation and she opened her eyes. Slowly she turned to locate her companion, who'd reared back and was gazing at her, appalled, and whose eyes now settled shut, on the downswing of the see-saw of consciousness they shared.

Reminded me of Jane talking about Nico the other night.

"You were doing her press?"

"No, I was trying to *manage* her! Musta been through John Cale, when I was with John. A few years before she died."

"She must've been in pretty bad shape already by then."

"Every morning she called me, woke me up, saying '*Jaaaaaaane*, it's *Niiiico*—'"

"In case you don't recognize the voice."

"'*Jaaaaaaane*, I vass at the *baaaaaaaaaaar* all *niiiiight*, and this man kept coming *ooooo*ver to my *stooooooool*. And in the *mooor*ning he stole my *booooooooooots*. And *Jaaaaaane*, I had all my money in my *booooooooots, Jaaaane*.'"

Every morning the same story, with the man and the stool and the boots."

"You had to know what you were letting yourself in for, no?"

"Well, she told me she was trying to get clean and she was on methadone . . . Which was true, but she was also on smack. That's the part she didn't tell me."

"Yeah."

"'*Jaaaaaane*, I don't know how I'll get *hooooome.*' Because she was living with me. '*Jaaaaaaane*, he stole my *booooooots*, I need *mooooooney*!' It was a nightmare."

•

We're at Film Forum waiting for a movie to start.

June is saying "When I was in my twenties I went to every movie. It was so exciting."

Two minutes ago I was telling her we should come see Satyajit Ray's Apu trilogy here in a few weeks, and all about the beauty of those films. Maybe it was two minutes. Now they're running a trailer for them.

She says "We should see this."

I can tell she's not connecting it with the films I just told her about. She doesn't listen to half of what I say—I'm always telling her about something.

She says "I'd really like to see this, Bun."

"This is what I was just telling you about."

She's looking at me.

She says "Well I want to see it too. Not just you."

Before it starts, she puts on her glasses. She sits straight up with her face in profile reflecting the screen, both feet on the floor, both hands holding the purse on her lap, chin raised, watching with the perfect attention of a dreamer, so that I can see in her that part of each of us that's reverential to narrative: here for a story, here for the show.

•

One night we were sitting on the rocks at the end of Grand Street, by the old Domino Sugar factory. The East River was sliding by, slapping up on the rocks in the wake of party boats. She said "No one's ever been this nice to me. Ever."

Across the water, cameras were flashing on top of the Empire State Building.

She said "Maybe some rich person will come along on Sunday and buy the place so we can be together whenever we want."

•

And what about these guys she got off the bus with in Santa Cruz? They got hold of some acid. What went on there?

Joe waves me over from a stationary bike. Not Father Joe—this Joe's an artist, a painter, teaches at Bard. Within moments, somehow, we're talking about food.

He says "I tried what Lou does with the *aglio olio*—"

"What's that?"

"You keep the water you boiled it in."

"I was doing that with the *cacio e pepe*. You use very little water and the water gets white, with the starch. And the starch helps the cheese stick to the pasta."

"Yeah, I didn't get it quite right. There must be a trick to it. I gotta ask him."

"You'll get it. There's always something."

He says "I'm still making adjustments to my mother's gravy. I only make it once or twice a year."

"With the meat, I cook the sauce in the oven. In a roasting pan. So it doesn't stick."

"Yeah?"

"You know the black enamel roasting pan? I brown the meat and lay it in there—the sausage, the spare ribs, whatever I'm using—braciole—and pour the sauce over. You cook it three hours, you don't have to stir it."

"*Really*," he says. "I gotta try that."

"All I heard when I was a kid—my old man: 'Stir the sauce, while you're up.'"

"Right. My mother. And you'd dip a crust of bread, while you were there."

"Right. So that's my innovation, the oven. That's my addition to the—y'know. To the literature for pasta. I only make it a few times a year, with the meat."

"I make it Christmas," he says.

"Alright," I tell him. "I'm going to Faicco's. I got June's brother coming over for his birthday."

"What're you making?"

"Pork chops with cherry peppers."

He okays that and keeps pedaling.

•

That coppery grey near the bottom of the sky . . . the color of a headache . . . where Broadway runs through the canyon of the buildings into forever . . .

•

O.K. UNIFORM CO. INC.   EST. 1938
253 CHURCH ST.   212-

•

June takes a break from packing, she's on the phone with Jane. Every year she works a big festival in Cannes. Not the film festival. This one's for corporate types who want to stay at Hotel du Cap so they can feel like movie stars. June's on the bed, slumped against the wall, chewing gum, blowing bubbles. She's killing time. It's one of these New York conversations you can't tell if she's bored or fascinated. It's a little of both. Bored fascination. Indifferent to the story, relishing the details. Jane's been cleaning out her closets.

"But wait a minute," June says. "The stuff you're finding, is it nice, or is it caca?"

Later she hands me the phone.

Jane says "And what are you going to be doing while your honey's away? Call me, I'll be right here."

"And you too. I'll cook you dinner. You shouldn't feel abandoned."

"*I won't*," she moans, as though sobbing.

"I'll call you this week."

"And you don't have to cook, we can go out."

"Sure."

"And we can go somewhere cheap and cheerful, you know, it doesn't have to be somewhere fancy-dancy."

•

June's in France, so Jane and I go for a walk to get dinner. At West Fourth and Bank there's a new hamburger place, a retro soda fountain with a marble counter and a tiled floor. Type of place you'd go for a black cow, or a ginger fizz. Every detail's perfect: the pressed-tin ceiling, the chrome fixtures, *Hamilton's Luncheonette* in 1940s cursive backward on the glass: it's like an art installation. The whole Village is now a museum of itself. But Jane's looking around, she remembers the room.

She says "Timothy Leary used to have this as a place, um. Where you could come—like if you were high? And you could lie down, there were mattresses, and candles, and there's quiet music, and it's very soothing, and Timothy Leary's going around in a white robe, making sure you're okay . . ."

"Like an opium den but for acid."

"But where you feel safe, and there's nothing scary."

"You came here to trip?"

"I think I did press for it for two weeks before the police shut it down."

While we're eating, I ask her "How do you do press for an illicit business?"

"It wasn't easy. You'd put the word out underground."

"Is that what you did with Woodstock?"

"Yeah."

"How, though?"

"Well. First of all, the newspapers didn't cover rock and roll. They did classical music and opera. And occasionally someone like Frank Sinatra or Doris Day or these old farts. But I had my list. I hadda read everything, every newspaper, every magazine, every one-page mimeograph from all over the country. And, um. I came up with about. I dunno. Three thousand names, on a list."

"List of who?"

"Of anyone who was doing anything to rock the system, anybody who ever, y'know, said anything progressive or said anything sympathetic about the counterculture. So for Woodstock, we sent out three thousand pieces of mail every night."

"Every *night*?"

"Every single night a different press release, for three months. We sat in the office after six o'clock, and we were usually there at three in the morning, because we had to address everything by hand. All night, addressing envelopes, stuffing envelopes, licking envelopes, stamping envelopes to get it to the post office."

"Seems like it worked out pretty well. What'd you get, half a million people?"

She burps and says "Pig!"

"Very nice," I hear June say.

Jane goes into her purse for a compact and reapplies her lipstick with a defiant flourish.

"Why does June disapprove of your doing that at the table?"

"She's very bossy, your girlfriend."

I can hear June: "One might consider using the restroom for something so personal. It's not nice."

Jane drops the compact in her purse. "Is my lipstick fucked up?"

"Perfect. You look like Klaus Nomi."

"That's what I was going for."

"What is that color?"

"Ugly Red."

•

In the parking lot of the Long Island City Costco at dusk, an old woman swaddled in a pink-and-blue sari is sitting on the tailgate of an SUV eating a peach and paying no mind while a young woman fits a pair of Day-Glo sneakers on her feet, fresh out of the box.

•

She was away for work, but I was going to her place anyway, walking up Seventh Avenue. It was late in the day, nearly

August, and block by block something in the light intensified, as though the world were trying to tell its secret, or as though everything meant more and more itself, verging on some sort of orgasm of wordless meaning, its best self, its absolute, and when I stopped for traffic at the corner of 12th Street that moment came—it came pouring in between the buildings with the light and the taxis on 12th Street, the day's exact climax, the moment when it meant something bigger than itself, something more than here, like God, or something more than now, like history, and I was there to see it and paying attention: I saw it happen.

And then I walked on.

I stopped into Westside Market and bought two cans of minced clams. Upstairs, I put a pot of water on the stove for pasta. When June and I took a trip to San Francisco—this was within our first few years together—I picked up a CD of Gene Clark's *White Light* demos, so I put that on. I set the big pan on the stove and drew a few loops of olive oil in it. I moved around the narrow kitchen, flicking shallot skin into the clean white sink; smashing garlic; opening drawers; turning a flame up or down; draining the milky clam juice into the pan while reserving the meat; measuring white wine; chopping parsley as the water increased its pitch, came to peak, and settled into a boil; dropping in a sheaf of linguine. When the pasta was drained, I tilted it from the colander into the pan and tossed it with the clams. I let it sit while I washed the pot and pan and put them in the rack. Then I fixed myself a shallow bowl and took it to the table by her big window. Down the hall, someone was practicing scales on a piano. There was still some light in the sky.

Sun orange below the bridges. That's how you know it's August: sun orange below the bridges at seven a.m., the way it lays itself on the streets. Now it commingles with the white fuselage of a Continental 737. I'm waiting on an early flight to Cleveland. My usual early-August trip.

Meanwhile, the usual asshole's on his phone, talking about his territory. A jet backing out, a luggage truck circling by, people moving past the glass toward the waiting area.

•

When I got to the airport I sent my stuff through the machine, phone and keys and coins. In the bin, right? But these new scanners you can't have anything in your pockets, metal or not. So I had to step out and send my wallet through, try again. TSA woman says "What's in your back pocket?" I reach for my bandanna—pull out a pair of panties.

Black lace panties with a little white pearl attached.

Which I then have to hold above my head. In the glass

cylinder. Like I'm under the mistletoe. While the scanner goes around.

You got a problem with that?

·

One brown whirly pod on the balcony. Helicopters, I think we called them. Autumn in the clouds at dawn.

·

On one of those trips I took my aunt out of the nursing home for ice cream. It was June's idea. Before I left New York, she suggested it. I explained the difficulty of getting my aunt into the car from her wheelchair.

"What about hiring a van? I think just to be in a parlor, and to make a decision, a cup or a cone, and what flavor, would let her feel a little independent for a change."

So I hired the van driver for the nursing home. We rolled the wheelchair into the back with my aunt sitting in it, and my mother and I followed in the car.

My aunt chose banana, which she didn't remember having had before, and was distressed at the size of the serving. We sat with the driver at a picnic table in front of the Honey Hut, as the breeze stirred in her hair and traffic blew by on State Road on a weekday afternoon.

•

A bale of compacted boxes behind a shopping center, pallets in the sun.

•

Pale sky over the Red Lobster. Long ago, David Loy's older brother had a big dirty silver Pontiac with a red velour interior. One evening we got in, Dave and Alex and I, and went driving around in a dusk of this same muffled light. I found a fifth of Seagram's under the seat and got loaded. In a carnival tent, they accused us of being pickpockets and threw us out, but not without a fight. The year for me is a continual recycling of microseasons and weathers and specificities of light I experienced before I was 20.

•

As we came in over Brooklyn I was at the window, trying to pick out her building across the river. Shadoobee.

•

Before the taxi's away from the curb, I call and get no answer. I'm back in my apartment before she calls.

"Where are you?" I ask her.

"Open the door."

And she's stepping off the elevator all in white denim, phone to her ear . . .

•

She got up to pull down the shade. "No one can see in," I told her. "It's bright out there and dark in here."

When I came, I came from so deep inside it felt like it was from a previous lifetime.

•

She's at the table in just a slip eating watermelon with a knife and fork, completely unaware of me.

•

Email to Tere:

Subject: THE MORBID JEALOUSY PLAYLIST

"Here we go, I'll spend a year now inventing scenes of her in bed with this guy and that one and playing them on repeat. Maybe two years.

Bed! Alleys and rooftops, more like. Airplane toilets, high above the Atlantic. Swinging between subway cars. On a bicycle. Generally I've got a half-assed imagination, but in this area, I'm gifted—I can really take off. Once you've been reactivated, all the world's a conspiracy of sex, you see it wherever you look. And not just now, but retroactively. Now that you're wired, you imagine everyone else is too, and has been all along. Why wouldn't any elevator ride lead to sex?

"It's not her boyfriends, let alone her husband. We all know what that's like. Nah, it's the spontaneous sex—the taking what you want—the *non*domestic, *non*programmatic sex that's so bewitching: backstage, back of a cab, downtown at dawn—the building she stepped out of at seven a.m. to go home and get ready for work."

•

June, eyes closed, says "Michael."

That's all. Not just saying my name but naming me.

•

The 6 came in you heard it with your fillings.

•

To Tere: "I call her at work it's like I'm talking to a different person. It's whiplash, from how she is on the weekend to how she is Monday, which is all business. On the weekend, I'm reassured by her tone, if not by what she says. During the week, I'm out here on my own again."

•

I had the day off but I met her outside the Y and we rode uptown, got some breakfast at Whole Foods. She'd been up since four in a panic about all the usual stuff and about having told me she'd take Friday off. Anyway, we crossed swords, and everything felt wrong between us when she went upstairs.

Of course I couldn't let it alone, I had to get off the train at 14th Street and call her. To make it right or make it worse—either way, I didn't care.

She said "I don't know if I can do this. You're asking me for something I can't give you."

And the next thing I knew I was crossing Sixth Avenue with the phone to my ear, saying "You want to call it a day?"

Back in Brooklyn I punched a hole in the bathroom door and sat in the corner of the couch looking at the sun in the dirt on the window.

•

Tonight she left me a message when I was at the gym. She said it's about her and not about us, but also that it's all one thing:

the separation and divorce, the apartment, where to move, me. She said she's been starved for twelve years and I'm giving her everything she was denied in her marriage. But she said that to be very frank, she feels like she's going from a marriage to another marriage, and it scares the hell out of her. She doesn't know what comes next and can't make any promises.

•

It was getting dark when I left the gym. I walked over to her block and called her back. While it rang I counted nine sets of windows up to theirs. The living room light was on, maybe the kitchen too.

She said "Where are you up to now?"

I said "I'm having a hard time with this."

He's home tonight but she made an excuse to come down. She's afraid he's going to find out about us and hire a lawyer, complicate the divorce. We went around the corner. It was dark now, and there was a breeze.

I said "I need something to go on."

She said "All I can tell you is I'm in it right now. I don't know anything about the future. Right now I'm trying to get out of something."

"I wish we never got started with this today."

She said "Nothing's changed. I've never felt any different."

Okay, I could go home with that. I went with her to the

Red Mango on 14th, to get her a frozen yogurt so she had something to walk back in the house with.

•

I woke up around five feeling hopeless but calm. At 7:45 I left, and rode the train into town. And while I waited there outside the Y, I remembered she doesn't want to be needed in this way. She says she likes this because it's easy and light and fun. Partly that's just her underplaying it. But I decided it's better she feel wanted than needed.

And then there she was on 14th Street with a smile. When we were on the platform she said she wasn't expecting me to show up. But she brought two nectarines.

•

And finally it's now again.

There's no high like when the pain eases off. The color gets dialed back into the world. It's like when you leave the dentist and you want to talk to every doorman, pet every dog, look at every flower. I had to stop myself from striking up a conversation with the guy beside me on the train. I don't know why. Nothing's settled. I'm like a teenager, an unstable substance. I want to make phone calls. But I can't think of anyone to call except her.

•

What was it about that corridor of a restaurant, with its multiplying floor tiles, and its wooden tables, and the owner talking in Italian with the cook about the price of a haircut for a dog, incredulous that anyone would pay to groom an animal, while the cook scrubbed something off the corner of the bar, and then the owner folded his arms and stood at the big window where *Ferdinando's Res Sicil* appeared in reverse in abraded gold letters and the late sun shone in the folds of an American flag outside that stirred and settled in the breeze?

A waiter, big young guy, bored, with nothing in the world to do until my order was ready, drifted past my table, leaned on the wall, noticed me, and said "What's that book?"

I started to tell him about it but he'd forgotten me already, looking out at the street.

•

Early in the morning and late in the day, the sunlight laid a thin film of sweat and memory on every surface. Piss rivulet across the sidewalk.

•

Nine a.m., guy in the Park Place subway station, shirtless, in shorts, soaking his feet in a plastic dish tub.

•

THE MORBID JEALOUSY PLAYLIST (continued)
"First you possess, then you're possessive. Then you're possessed. The scenes in my head—I've got them on a loop. A jealousy reel. To which I add a new clip when I hear a name I haven't heard before. Including guys I find out she met only in passing. Or whom I got mixed up with someone else. Or who turn out to be gay. Meanwhile she's just eating her breakfast. 'Waitaminute, *which* guy from Gang of Four?'

"I don't touch the subject. I don't press. I've got the sense to be embarrassed, at least. June herself is discreet and unapologetic about her past.

"Discreet, unapologetic: that's her to a *T*."

•

Since June moved into the Vermeer, I've been leaving Lou's magazines at the desk. Five *People*, five *Entertainment Weekly*. Plus whatever monthly. I get cryptic voice mails.

"Yeah, Mike, this is Lou, how you doing, Mike? Anyway, just wondering if you wanted me to go pick up those items. This afternoon, y'know, tonight sometime. It's up to you, whatever's easier for you. Doesn't matter to me. Aright. Let me know. Thanks Mike."

•

An immense man in a khaki suit—maybe four hundred pounds—in a splash of sidewalk light, glasses in hand, considering the menu of a Spanish-Chinese place on 14th Street.

•

Fire escape tomato plant. We've got five flowers now. The familiar first-thing clatter of the window gate reminds me of Kasia—when I lived downstairs from her and Tony on Grand Street—watering her windowboxes every morning, the water running through the planters and splashing, glittering through the fire escape, floor by floor. She's got two beautiful kids now with someone else, and Tony got married again last weekend near Woodstock. And I've been divorced and married again and divorced since then and now I'm with June, and June's been married and divorced and now she's with me. Sunday morning I pop out to water the tomato and the basil. There's a guy directly across the street, also in a white T-shirt, inspecting his plants. They say it's going to rain today, but they've been saying that for two weeks. There's a running reflection of the gutter on my ceiling from the hydrant across the street. Careful not to splash the lower shoots, I water the tomato till the water pools on the dirt, seeps in, and trickles through the rusted fire escape below.

•

"Did I tell you they finally accepted an offer on their place? A couple, two women. There've been others, but no one who met their asking price. Of course anything could happen. They still need approval from the bank and the board."

•

I took Lou a plastic container with four pork cutlets and a lemon. Told him I don't need the container. The next morning, he left it at the desk. Filled with pasta—elbows—from the bag. Didn't want to give it back empty. So today he's coming around the track, he sees me there, folds his newspaper. I thanked him for the pasta. "It's just under a pound," he's telling me, walking backward on the track, "the pound doesn't fit—"

"Thanks, Lou."

People are going around him. "The gomiti rigati, with the ridges!" I'm by the door, he has to shout. "Probably fifteen ounces almost, nearly a pound!"

"Okay, thanks, Lou."

"Eight minutes it's done."

•

"When I got to work I sent her a one-line email. I didn't even need a response, but pretty soon I'm checking my inbox— work, home—refreshing the screen. Then I start checking my phone for texts. By 11 a.m. and two iced mochas I'm climbing out of my skin. At noon I go walk around Rockefeller Center instead of refreshing my screens every minute like a speed freak.

"By 1:00 I'm convinced it's over, she's just waiting for the right time to let me know, and by 2:00 I'm congratulating myself on adjusting to life without her. Then I remember she has a meeting till 2:30, which is when she writes back.

"Okay, I'm a person who needs help. But email creates its own anxiety. The minute you send one you're waiting for a reply. Whoever it is. Let alone the person controlling your air supply. Email, texting, Facebook, WhatsApp and all the other forms of messaging—this is another thing they've sold us now: the anxiety of connection."

•

Lou's on the track this morning. Sees me, folds his paper, drops it on the pile. He's got a pile of stuff he keeps on the floor while he's going around. And from that pile he comes up with a plastic bag: a dozen elbows tied up with a big knot. It's what didn't fit in the container the other day. Because I should have the rest of the pound.

I go around with him. I ask what he's doing today, he says laundry. Philly goes by.

"Zulo Zul'!" Lou says.

"What'd you call him?"

"*Zulo zulo*: 'alone, alone.' On Elizabeth Street there was a guy, never married, lived there his whole life. And when he got drunk he was out on the stoop—'*Zulo zul'*! I'm *zulo zul'*!' That's Philly. He's in mourning because his woman left him. It's been six months."

"Well, it's understandable, Lou."

"He's a mamaluke."

•

"Strychnine" comes on, she's getting dressed, doing a little unconscious shuffle. Any of these bands, she perks right up: the Sonics, the Seeds, 13th Floor Elevators. It's like her body's paying attention.

She holds up a blouse on a hanger and sees me watching.

"Makes you feel happy," she says.

•

Guy playing catch with himself against a handball-court wall. Woman sitting on her walker with a cigarette in a housing project, watching the playground action.

•

"The other day she tells me about a Spinal Tap moment, when she led New Model Army, their tour manager, two roadies, a merch guy, Jane—eight people all trying to get to the dressing room—upstairs and down, through backstage tunnels, past a mop closet, and into the women's bathroom. Took 'em all into the bathroom, past stall, stall, stall, right to the end, where she was I guess expecting to find another door. ('The bottom line is I should never lead anyone anywhere.') To anyone else it's just a good story. But to me, it's another item on the tabloid news ticker that's always running in my head: 'NEW MODEL ARMY AFTER-SHOW ROMP . . . WELCOME TO LA: YOUR RIDE'S HERE . . . THREE IN A BED: SANTA CRUZ ACID PARTY SHOCKER!'"

•

She's got a red-carpet event tonight so I'm at La Taza de Oro, on Eighth Avenue. Like the A train, which I just got off, it feels like the past in here. The tired light of forty and fifty years ago, when Chelsea was Spanish. Maybe it's the light-box menu signs above, hand-painted in Spanish and English with the specials of the day: *Jueves/Thursday . . . Chuletas Fritas/Fried Pork Chops . . . Ensalada de Pulpo/Octopus Salad . . . Sopa de Carne/Beef Noodle Soup.* The counterman looks like a cornerman. He lifts his chin at me. When I tell him what I want, he fills a plastic tumbler with water, drops a fork and knife on a napkin, and turns away to the steam table.

The other morning June read me the obituary of a woman who quit nursing in her forties to follow a childhood dream of becoming an actress.

"Oh my God, Michael, that is so inspiring."

"Makes you want to quit your job, right?"

"Yes!"

"Anything inspiring always make me want to quit my job."

"But the only problem is, I didn't have a childhood dream. When I grew up I wanted to be a babysitter."

The counterman brings a plate of oxtails and a plate of yellow rice with pinto beans. While I eat I watch him work. End of the shift. He's emptying tumblers into the sink, he's cutting open a new bag of coffee beans, he's ladling soup, he's spooning yellow rice into a foil to-go container and flattening its crinkled edge around the lid with the back of a knife.

She said: "You're everything I prayed for when I was thirteen. I used to lie awake in my bed at night, and I was so lost, and belittled, and alone, and I used to—I don't know if I even knew I was praying, I was just—I had nothing. So the only thing I knew was to follow this fantasy or that fantasy: that was my only escape. Because everything was no. And no one would tell me why. 'Because I said so.' I wanted to take guitar lessons—'No. What do you need that for?' 'What am I supposed to do, just sit in my room?' I couldn't even put up a poster. 'Why not? It's my room.' Because they said so."

People are moving past the neon coffee cup in the window. With nerve and perseverance, she's gone from nothing to making twice what her father made in his best year. Twice what I make. She's out there somewhere tonight. My Brooklyn Bomber. My Coney Island baby.

To know if it's okay to take the plates, the counterman gives me a clipped umpire's gesture. I nod.

"Algo más?"

"Un café."

●

"Hey, Mike, this is Lou. I got the magazines: I got them about eight . . . eight fifteen, like—about eight thirty. But anyway . . . Don't stress yourself out with these magazines.

Don't go crazy . . . just whenever they're there, they're there, that's all. If you're early you're early, if you're late you're late, doesn't matter. Whenever I get 'em, whatever day, don't make any special trips, or—you overslept, or— Sleep! You need it! Awright, it worked out well. Just I appreciate it. But whenever I get 'em I get 'em! No problem. So. After I left the gym I picked 'em up . . . And that's that, I stayed home all day. Rained all day, what's the sense of going anywhere? Aright, thanks Mike. I'll be in touch."

•

I'm on the M train after work, we're crawling over the bridge, moving out past the projects and playgrounds and the FDR. The sky's overcast, but the change from afternoon to early evening comes filtered through, just a feeling. Something in the light reminds me of being young in the city. Any city, hot summer night. Leaving work with your shirt hanging open, the shirt you've been wearing all day. Out on the evening like we're out on this bridge—between stations. You're yourself again, on your own two legs, the air is yours to breathe. Watching yourself through the eyes of your hometown self. Now the real day starts—your portion of it, the real day—and it's forever, or enough time to do what matters: work on your novel, go to a rehearsal—pick up a half pint or a dime. You haven't lost the feeling that time is how you look at it. And there's no tomorrow, only tonight.

•

Lou runs into a guy he knows who's carrying a bag of laundry, walking with his wife.

Lou says "What're you doing?"

"I'm doing laundry."

"How come she doesn't do it?" Lou says.

"What century *you* living in?" the wife says.

He's telling me this at the Y. He says "Can you imagine those guys who came over here in the fifteenth century—men like Pizarro and Cortés—can you imagine those guys doing their own laundry?"

"It was the fifteenth century, like you say. And that's who we're looking at for correct behavior? Cortés? Who does your laundry?"

"I do."

"So?"

"I'm *zulo zul*," he says, throwing the upward chop that dismisses all dispute. "It's a different thing."

He follows me into my row buttoning his shirt.

"If you can take it," he says, "alone is better. When I was with Catherine, I come home, she made all kinda plans for us, we're going here, we gotta go there. Who needs it?"

Hector comes in from the gym.

"How's Philly?" he says.

"He's in mourning," Lou says. "He's mourning because his woman left him."

"Well," Hector says, "if my woman left me, I'd be sad also."

"He's a mamaluke. First class."

•

One morning in the summer we first got together, her hair was twirled above her head on the pillow like she was going up in flames.

"You're my secret weapon," she said. "You're my favorite thing. Anywhere. You're better than dark-chocolate ice cream, you're the best Rolling Stones song. Don't think for one minute that I don't know how lucky I am. Because I do."

"If you think you're the lucky one here, I've got you fooled."

"You know nothing."

"We're both lucky," I said. "Any two people who find each other are lucky."

"But we're luckier," she said. "Michael."

•

Always in the past I've been able to imagine an afterward. Now I can't. It's blank.

There's no after-June.

•

ALL-NIGHT BLOW PARTY IN POGUE'S HO-TEL ROOM . . . MSG BACKSTAGE ENCOUNTER, TRANSATLANTIC FLING! . . . CLOSE QUARTERS IN THAMES HOUSEBOAT!

•

Lou's talking to a guy in shorts with a long white ponytail and a walking stick. Not a cane but a staff. His name is Roy, he's 92 years old, still working. Lou introduces me, as he always does, as one of the top guys, a top writer. Roy's writing his fifteenth play. He teaches at the New School, Shakespeare and fiction.

Lou asks him the secret of his longevity.

Roy stops to think. As though he's just now considering the question after 92 years, he says "I don't know . . . I never drank much. Try to be careful about what I eat. And my wife takes very good care of me."

"You've got a wife!" Lou says. "You're lucky you're still alive! Usually men die younger when they've got a wife."

I've gotta laugh. "Well that's a—"

"You're wrong," Philly says, from his locker.

"That's one way to read the fact that women live longer."

"You're wrong anyway," Philly says. "Married men live longer."

"Zulo Zul'! You got no wife!"

"And I'm dying!"

"You're lucky to be free of that girl."

Philly says "Y'know, Lou, everything's not as simple for me as it is for you. You read an article, you eat a sandwich: you're happy. The simple pleasures are enough for you. They're not enough for me."

Lou, shaking his head, steps into his pants. Another man is making his way through. Puss like an undertaker.

"Wake up, Lou," he says.

•

It's been a hundred degrees, like a pizza parlor out there. At night it goes down to 92, the hydrants open, the curbs running, two cars double-parked with all their windows down pumping music, one salsa, one rap. You go to sleep with the fan blowing and wake up with the fan still blowing on the same day again.

•

"Morning, honey."

"What time is it, Michael?"

"It's about ten after five."

"I'm having a wonderful dream."

"Oh, sorry. You stay there."

"They changed Fifth Avenue. All the facades, back to the original way. And they're letting people go in and out, to see the houses."

"Okay, have fun."

•

Philly's band is playing on Christopher Street, a place called the 55 Bar. So June and I go down for the first set. It's early, 7:00—the sun is out—we sit at a table with Lou and Patsy and Hector from the Y.

Halfway through the set, I need to use the toilet. It just comes over me—I'm in a hurry. But it's one of those bars where the bathroom's behind the stage—you climb over the band—so I leave June at the table and go to her place. From Christopher Street, six or seven blocks, up Seventh Avenue. Takes me twenty minutes, there and back.

By which time the set's finished and June's out front. Guarded by Lou. And Patsy and Hector, his deputies. Lou won't leave her till I get back. Or let her go. So Patsy and Hector have to wait there too. Though they don't know what it's about, exactly, it's Lou's deal. June's telling Lou she lived her whole life in New York. Plus it's the West Village in 2012, not Avenue C thirty years ago. Plus it's only a few blocks. Plus the sun's in the sky. No can do: Lou's alert to the street, with Patsy and Hector sort of dozing off beside him. When I walk up, Lou hands her over. He says he'll see me in the morning and waves down a cab for Patsy. And Hector says he's gonna go.

•

Black sidewalk door propped open on cellar stairs. Garment racks on cobblestones.

•

"Thanks for asking, T. Things are good with June, except I had a dream last night about a shiny black monkey who was calling me, somewhat disrespectfully, I felt, 'Mister President,' and in response I BIT HER ON THE ARM in my sleep."

•

"How's dinner?" she said without opening her eyes.
 "Good! We just went to Elephant."
 "What'd you eat?"

"I had the spaghettini."

"You had that sundae, didn't you?" Eyes still closed.

"I had the sundae. The Carmen Miranda."

"That's not what it's called."

"The Lili St. Cyr."

"It's the Scarlett O'Hara. What Pete have?"

"Pete? Pete had a slimming salad and a modest slice of blueberry pie. Me? I ate half a loaf of bread and a big plate of pasta and topped it off with a hot-fudge sundae. For I am Gargantua. And I'm lumbering out of your forests to flatten your cities and set fire to your lakes."

•

"Tere, it comes on like chemicals or something. I go from elation to blackness and fear. I know she's busier than I am at work, so our experience of time is different. I know that. But I feel like a fish tossed up on a riverbank. Drowning in air. In the past hour alone, there've been sixty separate minutes when she hasn't called or written me back. If I can't stand it, how can she?"

•

"Yeah, Mike, this is Lou. I couldn't talk to you before because I was in the dentist. But anyway, so, sounds good, I can get those items tomorrow morning no problem. Aright. And, uh, I wanted to talk to you about that dinner! It was very good! And the price is right, and they give you good portions! It's unbelievable! Aright. —The chicken Parmesan is better than Gene's, 'cause it's bigger, crispier. Better— thicker. Very good. More authentic. Alright: later. I just polished off a pint of Talenti: it's a gelato. Delicious! Sicilian pistachio. I ate the whole pint. It's on sale at Whole Foods: three ninety-five. Usually it's like eight dollars a pint. So half the price. Problem is, you can't stop eating it. They got about ten flavors: caramel, sea salt, this, that. Peanut butter chocolate—so many flavors, but I stuck with that one. Alright! I'll be in touch."

●

Black ribbed sleeveless shirt, black miniskirt, high black boots. Full moon through fast-moving clouds. I grow fangs.

●

ON THE ROAD WITH BILLY BRAGG: TOUR BUS CONFESSIONS! . . . TWO EMPTY SEATS ON A FLIGHT TO DALLAS . . . MY NIGHT WITH THE DEAD BOYS!

•

I had to get a grip on myself before I drove her away. So I went uptown to talk to my friend Ken. I knew him in San Francisco, when we worked at the same place. Then he left to become a therapist and I lost touch with him. Ten years later I'm walking through the Rockefeller Center subway station and here he comes, with a new partner, Jens, and a practice in New York. And it was as natural as anything to run into him—in fact, this made me suspect that co-incidence doesn't surprise us. We pretend to be surprised because that's the convention, but deep inside, where we're in sync with the nature of things, we're unsurprised. Any-way, I went up to meet him at Fine & Schapiro, a kosher deli across from their apartment. But it turns out they're not supposed to have friends as clients. He said he'd give me a couple of names.

•

A cloudy August morning, "Diamond Dogs" comes on and it's early November. One of those overcast, windless days, like life in a diorama.

•

On the Rockaway ferry, we pass a small lighthouse.

"They built a lighthouse here on land?" she says.

"Lighthouse is always on land."

She's silent, looking out the window.

"That's the point of a lighthouse," I tell her, "to warn you where the land is."

She looks at me. Then she goes back to looking out the window.

"Where do you think a lighthouse should be?" I ask her.

"Don't speak to me." Then: "I'm not a seafaring person. I'm a city person."

•

I'm sitting with a plate of food on my lap in a house in New Jersey when a photo album comes my way. And there's a picture of June, maybe 12 or 13, from a wedding or bar mitzvah. Taller than her cousins, pale, peculiar, dark circles around her eyes. Someone has put her in a ridiculous pale-blue party gown and yanked her hair into an approximately presentable style.

There's really no sign that in a few years she's on a bus to California and this is all fading behind the green Pennsylvania mountains. Or no sign except that she's so out of place.

Once I asked her why, in every picture of her as a kid, her hair's been straightened and chopped in bangs.

"All they knew how to do was compare us to everyone else. And they knew that I didn't look like everybody else. My mother would get out the scissors and chop it off. And at the time when I was growing up in the seventies: *straight hair*. I was just this tall, gawky, frizzy-haired *freak*, in my parents' eyes, listening to music."

When I got to know her family, I couldn't see much of them in her. She's self-created. She's the girl in the Lou Reed song whose life was saved by rock and roll.

In that party picture, she's looking right at you. You can see she's stranded there, an embarrassment, with no awareness that fitting in here will turn out to be the last thing she wants. That life isn't like this. That her real life is out there, waiting for her.

•

The sky had gotten darker. Sunday afternoon, all the windows were open wide. I've realized only lately how happy I can be just watching her. Going about her business. There's something mysterious about it. Every once in a while I notice that she isn't me. She was standing at the window with her arms folded. There was a crack of thunder, a crack and then a roll. She looked up, looked down. Then the rain came straight down all at once. She had her hair up, her glasses on. She bent to see under the open window, and I could tell she was sniffing the air at the screen. She straightened up. She caught me watching and she was self-conscious. "The rain smells sweet! Can you smell it?" Then she went back to watching, arms still folded, alert to its magic, in this never-to-be-repeated afternoon of her one life.

•

Philly was on one of the couches by himself. Something about him caught my attention, a quietness. I walked over.

"Philly."

He stood up. "Hey, pal." He had a sad little smile.

"You okay?"

"Aah, I got girl trouble," he said. He was quite altered.

"Anything you want to talk about?"

"Nah," he said. "Thanks for asking." Then he walked off toward the stairs.

I remembered a morning when he came in talking about their night at the Carlyle.

"Made a reservation in the name of Dr. Frederick Sherman," he said. "When I go to restaurants uptown I always pose as a doctor."

"Doctor Philly."

"That's right. This way they all make a fuss over me— 'Your table is ready, Dr. Sherman.'"

They went to see Bettye LaVette, it cost him nearly $500.

He said it was worth it. The Bemelmans Bar, where they went first for a drink (martini: $18), was the greatest place in New York, and Bettye LaVette was the greatest soul singer in the world, better than Aretha, better than anyone you could name. For dinner he had Dover sole ($65).

That same morning, I got on a stair machine next to Lou.

I said "Philly had a good time at the Carlyle the other night."

"That's a class joint," Lou said, while reading the *Post.* "If you ever wanna impress a broad, that's the place to go."

"Expensive," I said. "He paid sixty-five dollars for a plate of fish."

"Dover sole," Lou said.

"That was a four-hundred-dollar night for him."

"Four sixty-five," Lou said, turning the page.

•

THE JUNE AND JANE SHOW

In a Town Car, Times Square, six p.m.: Jane up front with her driver, Pedro, June and me in back . . .

JANE: Joe [*Sicari, her neighbor*] called me the other night he wants to go for a walk. So we walked . . . along West 12th Street to Hudson and then back again, and then he decided we should go to Good Stuff Diner, and then I got very angry at Good Stuff so we left Good Stuff—

JUNE [*laughing*]: Why did you get angry?

JANE: Because—I spend a lot of money in there. I really do. And there was nobody in there. And, um. And I know they get very crowded around two or three because there are clubs around there and they've already had three shootings. But it's too early for them, and lots of booths and tables and everything, so Joe says "We're just gonna have a cup of coffee." So the man says "Would you like to have a cup of coffee at a table by the window?" I said "No I'd like to have a cup of coffee in a booth."

JUNE: Yeah.

JANE: And he didn't want us to sit at the booth so I just said "I'm leaving, goodbye. Have a good time with—"

JUNE: So what'd you guys do instead?

JANE: *So.* Then Joe said "Why don't we go in the Donut Pub?" and I said "Okay, let's do that."

JUNE: Ohhhh no . . .

JANE: I'm still on the No Donut Diet, don't worry. But—

JUNE: *But* you did manage to eat what?

JANE: Nothing, no no. But, in the Donut Pub now, there's a man, an older man, and he's in there doing magic tricks for everybody and he's got these puzzles on the counter, and . . .

MIKE: I've seen him in there.

JUNE: So you're going to the Donut Pub too now?

MIKE: I like to keep abreast of developments in—

JUNE: When were you in there?

MIKE: I was in there with Pete or something. And this magician was there.

JANE: He's really good. And he's really sweet. But he twawks like dis, y'know, he's got that very Bronx— I can't even do it, but I mean it's really thick. And—he's *very* smart, and very very clever and he makes up a lot of these things. But he's also trying to sell them, he—

MIKE: Puzzles, right? Little wooden puzzles.

JANE: Yeah, also he has little pieces of plastic, and then he's got this other thing where you make a pyramid out of all these different pieces . . .

MIKE: Right, right.

JANE: But I mean it's *impossible*. So, little by little people are coming in—everybody's playing these games, and now everybody's trying to share information—

JUNE: [*Laughter*]

JANE: —"How do ya do this?"—

MIKE: [*Laughter*]

JUNE: How *fabulous* is that? It's *so*— It's like a real moment.

JANE: Yeah! A New York moment, absolutely. But I mean it's a riot because everybody from every kind of walk of life comes in and he somehow engages each one of 'em, and they're all playing with his stuff and all talking to

one another: "Well, did *you* do this one? *I* can't do it—
what'd he say to you?" And the police they came: "Sean!
C'mon!"

JUNE: [*Laughter*]

MIKE: The cops were playing too?

JANE: *Yeah*, the cops know him, everybody knows him, I
mean he's a very—

JUNE: I wonder if I've seen him, if I—

JANE: I think you would know him, he's not, y'know, he's
not exactly a looker— And, y'know, he's got the kind of
face you'd kinda remember?

MIKE: Does he dress in a particular way?

JANE: Yeah. Terrible. He had some kind of a black T-shirt?
and black pants, and nothing fit right, y'know—

MIKE: But he's not dressed like a magician or anything.

JANE: No no.

MIKE: And how does he get any money? If somebody buys
a puzzle, or do you give him a tip?

JANE: You can leave a tip in his tip jar, but he doesn't hassle
you—"And don't forget to leave a tip" every five minutes,
nonea that. Y'know. And he tries to sell his puzzles. But
he doesn't tell you fifteen times.

MIKE: Right, right.

JANE: And um. And the puzzles are kinda great. And *very*
hard, but—I could do one but that's 'cause I cheated.

JUNE: How do you cheat?

JANE: Well, because I watched someone else *do* it, and then he *showed* me, and then I hadda look *again*, I mean—it's—even when someone shows you one of these puzzles, it's not like you can remember for two seconds how they do it. I mean it's just— For my brain— I don't have that kind of . . . It's just too advanced, the—putting together pieces that fit together in different ways—I mean it just—makes me wanna scream, kill myself.

MIKE: And it's usually something obvious.

JANE: Very obvious! And then in two seconds he shows you the whole thing—and you say "Oh my *God*, is that all it is?" And then you don't even *remember* what he showed you.

MIKE: Yeah. But *this* is what I like about this story, 'cause Joe calls her at like—

JANE: [*Laughter*]

MIKE: —at 10:30 to go for a walk: he can't get to sleep—

JUNE: Right, right.

MIKE: —he's been alone all day—so they start out walking—just anywhere, right?

JANE [*laughing*]: Yeah. And then he still wasn't ready to go home. I think he just wanted to prolong the walk. Which is probably why he—"Well let's go to the Donut Pub!" But it was fantastic. Now he's best friends with this guy and he learned how to do some magic tricks, which are really—

MIKE: Who, Joe?

JANE: Yes! He learned, I think, two card tricks last night that are unbelievable. And he learned how to do the pyramid puzzle which, forget it. I mean I saw it done forty-five times I still can't do it.

JUNE: You must've had the best—so much fun. So many laughs.

JANE: It was. It was a lot of fun.

JUNE: Just like old New York. That's so fabulous, Janie.

JANE [*getting a little bored with the topic*]: Ycah . . . Right . . .

JUNE: Good for you. Remember when those—that used to happen . . . more frequently? The way that everything just sort of always connected, and one step led to another?

MIKE: Spontaneous.

JANE [*preoccupied*]: It was great, it was so much fun . . .

MIKE: So were you there how late?

JANE: We were there till about one fifteen maybe? Or something like that.

JUNE: How fabulous.

MIKE: We gotta get together with Joe. He's going to show us how to make those Italian cookies. With sesame seeds.

JANE: Yeah he *wants* to very badly, he's dying to have a dinner, make a dinner . . .

•

Small yellow sun reflected in the front quarter panel of an old green truck idling at a light.

•

Ronkonkoma
Wantaugh
Speonk

•

Thursday after work we're in the scrimmage at Penn Station, eyes on the board so we can jockey to the stairs and jostle our stuff down to the train and drag it across the platform at Babylon and onto the Bay Shore train and then haul it to the shuttle and pile it on the ferry dock—a suitcase, a bag of groceries, a bread, two cooler bags containing eight bronzini I froze and forty pork cutlets from Faicco—and load it on the ferry to Ocean Bay Park. Every summer Jane rents a house on Fire Island for a month. She stays out there, the rest of us come and go.

Now we're on the top deck, June and I. As the boat picks up speed and foam peels off the hull, we're reading a paper someone left behind—the obituaries.

"If you ever place an obituary for me," she says, "don't put my age in it. Leave that out."

"Even when you're dead, no one should know your age?"

"That's right. No one should know that. Ever. No one needs to know that."

"Really? I always tell people how old you are."

"What do you say?"

"I say 'I'm having dinner with June. She's fifty-two, you know.'"

"No. Don't say that."

"People say 'What'd you do this weekend?' I say 'I went to the movies with my older girlfriend.'"

"Don't ever say that. If someone asks—"

"They don't ask. I volunteer."

"I know you do. From now on, you say 'I'm not sure exactly. She's in her early fifties.' That's all you have to say. From now on. From now until I die."

"Got it. 'She was born in the early fifties.'"

"No."

"'I'm not sure exactly. I know she was born in the fifties. The *early* fifties.'"

"I'm gonna hurt you. In your sleep, I'll hurt you. I'll shave off all your hair."

"Don't you worry. 'She was born sometime back in the early fifties.'"

"Your eyebrows. How'd you like that?"

·

Stars through pine branches, the unbroken insect screel like fishing line running out of a reel.

·

That time June suggested Fire Island as a chance for Jane to start clearing out the dead friends and relations whose ashes were in her closet. Not in urns but in plastic bread bags, un-named. We took a bag down to the beach in the dark and I caught a face full of ash and bone shards that BG tossed into the wind. Jane thought it might be Lenny Baron. Definitely wasn't John Vogel, whose remains she'd sprinkled, a little at a time, in Bloomingdale's and Saks. Going up and down the escalators.

·

Meanwhile, back in the city that first summer, she let me know that after the place sells, she's going to stay with Jane, across the street. I told Tere: "Maybe she's clearing some space for herself. Some room to breathe."

·

Lemon-ice sky, greyblack bay as we walk to the dock to meet Bobbie and Dara. And as we're coming back with the wagons, golden light under greyblue clouds.

•

Someone posts a clip on Facebook of a woman with her arms locked around an eighty-pound wombat. She lugs it around, its belly exposed. I call June over.

"That's a stuffed animal," she says.

"It's a wombat."

She stares at the screen without expression as the creature allows itself to be trundled around in a wheelbarrow.

"No," she decides. And gets off the couch.

•

That time a big white Lab wandered into the yard and we called the number on its tag and left a message, and before we heard back, the dog wandered out again, and BG, mortally afraid of ticks, followed it saying, unpersuasively, "Here, honey; here, sweetheart," walking parallel to it on the sidewalk as it moped and sniffed through the brush nearly all the way to Ocean Beach, "Here, sweetie; here, honey," before we caught up with them and June marched into the weeds and grabbed its collar . . .

•

After our sunrise visit to the beach, we take the sandy wooden stairs. June in her white jean jacket and pajama bottoms, barefoot. Jane in her Ramones T-shirt and tartan shorts, barefoot. They go on ahead, close in conversation, paying no attention to anything else. I stop to look at a pine branch beside the walk. Needles and small cones are standing out in a yellow concentration of the water-clear light of this hour.

Reminds me of Northern California: pine branches warming in early sun, a blue sky beyond. So it's not just this pine I'm seeing, and it's not just today. This light has a keen edge of meaning for me because it's underscored by time the way a movie scene is underscored by music. In this case, the music of experience.

Back at the house, Jane's busy reading the news on her AOL page instead of the 75,000 unread emails in her inbox while June pours water into the coffeemaker.

•

Coffee. The rising chatter and the unspooling sound of insects. Leaf and windowscreen shadows on the pages of the book I'm reading. A cardinal answering his own questions.

•

Every morning at Fire Island, June and I walk on the beach to watch the sun come up. We started taking a plastic bag. As we go, we fill it with trash. Water bottles, beer cups, Mylar balloons from parties. The balloons we pop to get more in the bag.

After a week of this we go past a couple of kids under a blanket.

"You know what they're saying?" I asked her.

"What?"

"They're saying 'Look, there's that weird old couple who go down the beach popping children's balloons."

·

That time we busted Jane in the dark in her plaid shorts, with her hair standing up, toasting a marshmallow on the stove.

·

Late in August, late in the day, and silvery sun in the curl of a wave before it breaks.

"This is the kind of day that reminds you you're going to die."

"What's on me?" she says, turning in circles to see her ass. "Did I sit in something?"

"Yeah, I'm afraid so."

"What is it?"

"I can't tell."

"I'm very unhappy, Mike!"

•

The world is rustling all around us.

•

One morning we walk to town, Ocean Beach. There's a dozen guys on a bench in front of the bakery. Shooting the breeze. All in shorts, all comprehensively tanned. They look like mob guys, or ex-cops. June wants to take their picture, she works up the nerve to ask. One guy jumps up, moves off. The rest are in high spirits, they tell her to fire away. She thanks them when she's done. They tell her if she comes back, they'll be on the bench right across from this one. They move with the sun.

•

We walk on the sand as the waves dump themselves on the beach and pull back, overturning shingle. The ocean puts you in touch with your death wish. That yearning for infinity. It satisfies your need to disintegrate and disperse. To be diffuse. We watch a wave's reflection in the sand as it's overtaken by the wave. There's a sandpiper at work. It chases the outgoing shine and flees the incoming foam. This is its anxious beat: it works the disappearing zone of reflection in the sand, the forever-vanishing now.

•

"Hey Mike. Boy, these weeks go by fast, ah? It's that time of the week already, Thursday. Aright, lemme know what's going on, if you want me to pick this stuff up. Send me some direction. Aright Mike, take care Mike. Thanks."

•

Way down the beach, a girl in a white sundress . . .

On Driggs Avenue, "Maggie May" was coming out the window of one of the cars at a light, and it reopened a place inside me: part imagination, part memory. Part ache for a time after which you never feel life quite so sharply again. The everlasting September. The mandolin player took his extra half measure—the very moment when summer ends, that last of it, after Labor Day. I cut between cars and could hear him hanging on: he held this glistening moment captive in a repeated phrase. And finally— after the band came back in and he knew the spell was slipping—he started changing it up, trying one thing and another to hold time still as the song moved on. Up over Metropolitan, a flight of pigeons flashed and turned.

•

"Tere, I quit drinking caffeine at night. But I still sit up smoking cigarettes and staring holes in the dark till I find something hopeful in something she said.

"She can't commit to anything except specific activities.

A trip to the shore, that new place on Grand. She wants to go to the Sheep & Wool Festival in Rhinebeck next month. So we're cool through the third week in October.

"She won't even say she's with me. It's not that I need to hear it so much as I wonder what keeps her from saying it. I told you when she sells her place she's moving in with Jane, right? While she looks for something to buy. Sure, she can stay at my place whenever she wants. But she won't move in with me. How do I explain that to myself?"

•

A cloud of furling dust in the open top of a compound bucket that a construction worker has put down after emptying it into a dumpster.

•

Lou folds up his newspaper when he sees me. His T-shirt's so threadbare it's transparent. They talked to him about it—there've been complaints—but he doesn't see it. Far as he's concerned, there's some life left in this shirt. I wind up going around five times with him. Some reason he's thinking about Dean Martin today.

He says "Dino was on a bill with Sinatra at the Westchester Theater, so we all went up. I saw Sinatra with everybody,

Ella Fitzgerald, Count Basie, but now he's with Dino, everybody wants tickets."

"Westchester? Why up there?"

"Westchester Premier Theater, in Tarrytown. Tony Dime had a piece of it, he was a wiseguy, did two years over the place. He says 'Come on, we'll eat first'—you could eat there too: place was a gold mine. They took so much money outa there before they got caught. Anyway, see the show, Tony says 'Come on backstage, meet Frank.' I said 'Tell ya the truth, I rather meet Dean.' He said—" Here Lou wagged the metronome, no-can-do finger of doom: "'Nobody sees Dean. Nobody. The limousine picks him up at noon, he plays golf alone, he eats alone, backstage he's got a room to himself.'"

"You met Sinatra instead?"

"Oh. Lots of times. And I saw him play thirty shows, after he came back in '73. Twice a year, I saw him."

"Here?"

"Here, Vegas."

We go half a lap in silence.

I tell him "Dylan made a record of Sinatra songs."

"Who?"

You have to say it twice, if you open a new subject with him.

"Bob Dylan."

"I read that. Not the greatest voice, but he has it here,"

he says, tapping his heart. "The greatest singers don't always have the greatest voices. They have it here. I met him one time, at Jerry Orbach's place."

"What, in the seventies?"

"Yeah, seventies sometime. Good guy, nice guy. Didn't say nothing, just sat in the corner, kept to himself. He asked me about Joe Gallo. Because he was writing that song about him."

Later, in the showers, he's talking about Perry Como— Mr. Relaxation: "The man who invented casual. He came along at the right time. He was perfect for TV like Bing Crosby was perfect for radio. Perry Como's personality wasn't too big. So he's perfect for Middle America. Because he's right in your living room, y'know. So Sammy Davis Junior, even Sinatra—they're too big for your living room. They're nightclub singers. But who's gonna buy a ticket to see Perry Como? He'll put you to sleep."

While we're drying off, he demonstrates Perry Como's deceptively easy style, with men moving around us in the tiled room: *"With a song in my heart, I behold your adorable face . . ."*

•

She stood at the crosswalk twirling one of her curls around a finger.

PARKING GARAGE

OPEN 24 HOURS

ENTER

•

"Philly, where was the Five Spot?"

"What?"

"The Five Spot. Where was it?"

"I think it was Bowery, near Cooper Square. I'm not sure, I never went to the Five Spot."

"No? Before your time?"

"I used to go to a club called Slugs'—on East Third, between B and C."

"When was that?"

"Nineteen sixty-eight. 'Cause I just got outa the Army. I went there—in a dashiki. Can you believe that? And shades and a little kufi. Pharoah Sanders was looking at me like *Who's this white guy coming here in a dashiki?*"

"That's not a big stretch, for you."

He said "I used to go there to see Roland Kirk. You know about Roland Kirk?"

"Yeah. Whistleman."

"Yeah! You know what Roland Kirk would do at the

Village Vanguard? He'd come off the stage, still playing—he was blind! he had a guy to lead him—and he'd go through the audience up the stairs, out on Seventh Avenue, still playing—people outside going, *What the fuck is this?* And he'd come back down the stairs, get back onstage and finish the show."

•

"Today I'm talking to Andrea at work about June when she ventures to ask if I've ever considered seeing someone.

"It's the delicate approach that lets you know how far you've strayed. The bedside manner. This is you, Ken Pound, Tony, and now Andrea who've suggested I seek professional help. And a lady in the cafeteria. Plus the breakers on the L train and a deaf guy handing out cards. I turned one over it said 'Get some help, willya?'"

•

Eight a.m., Steve's crossing Seventh Avenue—homeless guy sits by the subway, outside the Vermeer. Says he got picked up by the cops last night for sitting too close to the stairs.

"Transit cops?"

"Transit cops, yeah. They said it wasn't ten feet. I was locked up all day, so I couldn't make no money. Which means I didn't sleep, because I couldn't pay for my room last night. I understand they got a job to do, but they took my milk crate, they took my cushion. Plus it was my birthday."

"Happy birthday. At least you're not waking up today fucked up, or hungover. Both of us."

"Right," he said. "Not knowing where you are."

"Who you are."

"What you did. My worst ever was I smoked what I thought was a joint, but it was laced. I woke up three days later in Florida, with a knot like *this* in my pocket with blood on it, and no idea what happened. I don't like that."

"No."

"First thing I did I went to the bathroom and washed off the top three bills, bought a bus ticket back to New York, and dropped the knot in a panhandler's cup to get rid of it. Never did find out what happened."

•

"What are you eating?" I asked her.

"Licorice."

"From where?"

"Downstairs."

"Okay."

"What else?"

•

Taxi driver praying with his shoes beside him on a piece of cardboard by his cab in Midtown.

•

"Feel like going to the movies tonight?" I ask her, out of the blue.

"Yes, Michael, I do," she says, as though she thought I'd never ask. "Don't you?"

"Of course you do. 'Tickle me, do I not laugh? Prick me, do I not bleed?'"

"Yes! Yes and yes."

•

Standing on the corner of West 8th Street and Sixth Avenue: traffic stops, the night bristles with shadows, the crosswalk comes alive. Everyone's out and moving around. There's a lot coming at you all the time here. Everything's unexpected, everyone's a surprise. New York is just so much more *information*—on a moment-by-moment basis—that it fires your synapses more than other places do. So you're literally more alive here, or at least more conscious. And there's a music to all this. I can hear it now while I'm waiting to cross 14th, in the old, warm, friendly world.

•

Two guys went past me on the track and in the break between two songs on my headphones I heard "Linguine?"

"No, fettucine."

•

We were out walking on the west side. On 20th Street, the
leaves had that golden glow of the translucent green grapes
in Dutch still lifes: an inner smile. Near Tenth Avenue, we
looked in on the seminary grounds. The seminary's a hotel
now. Or part of it is. You can't go in there anymore.

She said "On a morning like this, when I was married, I
would come over and sit on a bench in there. And I was so
alone. I was so sad. I did all the right things, I tried so hard, I
did every— I put myself in a box. I made myself smaller and
smaller until I could fit in this little box. And it still wasn't
enough. It was never enough. And I used to sit here and think
What a beautiful world. What have I gotten myself into?"

•

June's on my bed with a book. On my recommendation,
she's been reading *Masters of Atlantis*, a Charles Portis novel

about a crew of hopeless clucks who start a pseudomystical fraternal order. One of the funniest books I've read. She's reading it stone-faced, like she needs to find out what's going to happen to these people. She'd no more laugh at them than she'd laugh at real people. She claims to have no sense of humor, though I feel like she might have a stronger sense of reality than I do.

But finally I have to ask: "How can you not laugh at that book?"

"I don't know," she says. "I feel bad for them. I want them to win."

She doesn't have an ironic bone in her body. I think she associates irony with bullying. Really, she's allergic to anything exclusive. The other day someone mentioned the band Jethro Tull and she frowned and wrinkled her nose. When I laughed, she said "I didn't like anything about that band, they were always a boy band, something just for boys." She said it with the same distaste she showed for anything trainspotterish. It's why she likes garage bands, and why she immediately responded to punk, when it came along: the Dolls, the Ramones were for everybody, not just the pretty kids, not just the popular kids, not just the smart kids, not just boys, not just girls. Prog bands were inconsequential to her not just because they were pretentious and unsexy and mostly the product of cloistered, ingrown intelligence, and irrelevant to anyone's experience, but because they were exclusionary. They offended her deep-seated Canarsie sense of democracy.

•

About a year ago I went into the showers, there was a big lump of a guy on a white plastic stool, obese, the water blasting on his neck, arms hanging between his legs like it was the end of the line. He lifted his face to the water, it ran out of his mouth. Then an old man came in and started soaping him down. He was only as tall standing as the other one seated. A barrel of a guy, like a wrestler. He soaped the other across the shoulders and under the arms. Got him up and soaped his ass with a washcloth. The big one put a foot on the stool and allowed the old man to clean under the folds of his fat and around his groin . . .

Today Lou pointed out the big one in the locker room, said he was Mateo's son, that Mateo's a beautiful guy and the son's his cross.

"Eats all day," Lou says. "He weighs five hundred pounds. Ever since they put him on the medication. He can barely get up the stairs. Mateo waits for him at every landing."

At the sinks, the son was plopped on a stool, letting his father shave him. They were both lathered up, steam rising from the sink. Mateo was shaving them both with the same razor, and only when his father leaned past him to rinse it did the boy king drum his fingers on his knee, just once, to signal the impatience he must have felt while undergoing, for his father's sake, the mysterious procedure.

•

"We got together Friday and Saturday. Then yesterday we went to the movies. Her husband started a new job, working days. So we won't be able to see each other as much. She reminds me it's not forever, and everything between us is good. But when things are good I worry. Sunday without her was a torment of anxiety.

"I feel like Larry Talbot. The wolfman. One minute I'm good. Then I feel it coming on: *Oh, no, it's happening again . . .*"

•

Today, Philly's wearing a black guayabera, pale-yellow slacks, and a pair of PR domino-player shoes, woven leather.

Hector, who's Puerto Rican, points to the shoes and says "Those are nice."

"They were nice when I got 'em. I've had 'em for years. Paul Stuart. You ever been in there, Paul Stuart? "

"There used to be an actor, Paul Stewart."

"You're right! You're probably the only guy here remembers him."

"You know what I saw the other night? With Humphrey Bogart and Ava Gardner—Bogart plays a movie director—"

"Right, with Edmond O'Brien. I can't think of the name."

"*Barefoot Contessa*," I put in.

"That's right," Philly says. "It doesn't hold up. You know what I saw the other night? *City for Conquest*. Remember *City for Conquest*?"

"Sure," Hector says.

"You ever see that, Mikey?"

"That's Cagney and Ann Sheridan? The brother's a composer?"

"Right!"

"Cagney's a fighter, supports his brother."

From the next row, Lou says "She had that extra something, Ann Sheridan. That verve or something." This is after he changed his locker, during a period of not speaking to Philly.

Philly says "At the end, Cagney's at the newsstand. He hears his brother's concert on the radio."

"Yeah," I remember. "And he sees Ann Sheridan again."

"That's right," Philly says. "He's blind, but he knows it's her."

"He says 'Looks like everybody from Forsyth Street's doing alright.'"

•

A moment of synesthesia: while I'm waiting for you here, I'm looking through this notebook. I see a description of what you're wearing and I smell your perfume. Which persists after I close the notebook, so that I'm sure you must be just about to arrive.

•

THE JUNE AND JANE SHOW

JANE: She used to stop traffic on Canal Street, this one. With her skimpy clothes. Skirts that barely covered her *tuchas*, legs a mile long, six-inch heels. In the middle of the afternoon. Leather pants that lace up the side. And she'd say [*switching to the high-pitched voice of indignation she uses to mimic June*]: "What's wrong with everybody?! What's everybody looking at?!"

JUNE: I don't sound like that.

JANE: "Why are they stopped? Why don't they go?"

JUNE: I don't *sound* like that!

JANE: "Why's everybody looking at me?!"

•

She made it there just as the reading was about to start, straight from work and dressed differently from anyone in the room, red lipstick and a short dress and black nylons and heels—I mean, she looked spectacular, but I knew it made her more self-conscious in a place where she already felt she didn't fit in. It wasn't a reading in a bar, it was Dia Chelsea: elevator to the fifth floor, white walls, grey cement floor, metal folding chairs, no amenities, the microphone at a lectern in a circle of white light. She came in just before it started with a bag of four apples, a dozen eggs, and a can of sardines she bought on her lunch hour and tried to make it to the seat beside me unnoticed.

The first reader was an academic. In a dismissive voice, he delivered the usual barrage of cryptic non sequiturs. Anywhere you went, all you had to do was open a tap and out came this same poem. June leaned over and whispered, anxiously, "Do you understand what he's saying?" I was already annoyed with the guy for wasting our time. But I hated him for making her feel stupid when, after a long day at work, she'd come to a poetry reading in the hopes of hearing something she could relate to.

"It's just about the sound of the words," I told her.

"But there are people laughing in the front row."

"They're here with him. It's not you."

"Are you sure?"

"Yeah."

"You're not just saying that?"

"I promise you."

The next reader, on the other hand, was operating in good faith, trying to communicate something besides his own boredom. There was life in his work. June bought three of his books and took one of them up for him to sign. The crowd had drifted out. I watched the two of them from my seat. No one had showed her the way to anything, she'd had to find it on her own. The poet was telling her about India. He asked her about herself. To June, this poet was more glamorous than any rock star. The other books were on a chair with her purse. She was embarrassed to hand him all three. Again I wished I'd known her since she was 14.

●

Last night she calls from the back of a cab after drinks with Steph, giddy and high, to say I make her knees go weak.

"We're going through Times Square, and I look out and—" Then she sighs. She says "I don't know what to do with this. This doesn't happen to me, it happens to people in movies, and Cinderella."

"Dig it!"

"I'm trying—I'm trying to adjust. You've been so patient. But look where we are—compared to where we were!"

●

Today is the world's bright day: all its buttons and buckles are shining. Before work I'm on a bench outside the Time & Life Building, unwrapping a French pastry she got me this morning, not too sweet, with a few raisins, tearing off a piece while a breeze like unmerited favor plays on my face and what's left of my hair.

•

Young guy with a backpack in a black suit and a loosened tie, waiting to pay for a wedge of chocolate layer cake in a plastic clamshell.

•

We close our phones at 9:20 but that doesn't stop the signals we're sending. They keep going, into the night, into space.

Later, I'm already reaching for the phone before I hear it ring.

"Are you awake?" she says.

"Yeah, I'm up."

•

The hot metal musk of the subway on a rainy morning. You are coming.

•

She was meeting me at a tailor on Washington Street. My phone rang.

"I'm a little turned around," she said. "I'm on Hudson and Horatio."

Lived her whole life in New York, but when it comes to directions, she's always wrong. I told her to walk toward the river on Horatio. Then I went to the corner and waited.

It was a nothing Saturday. There was no one around. But pretty soon she came along, across the street. She had her hair pushed up under a floppy cap—black and white checks—and she was halfway up the block before she saw me and started laughing. She was the only person on the street, so anyone looking out the window would have figured she's crazy. Right then she did seem a little zany, even to me. But with everything I could want in a woman—the spark, the joy, the innocence. The party spirit. I wished my father could have met her. I wished he could have seen her walking up that red-brick street, laughing at life.

•

I was tying my shoes. I heard one guy and then another ask Lou how he's doing. His voice was different.

I went to his locker. "What's going on?"

He shrugged. "My brother's sick, they called me. I don't know why they waited. I coulda gone up there."

"You mean he's that sick? Is he conscious?"

He shrugged again.

"How old is he, Lou? What's his name?"

"Paulie. He's seventy-four. Which is nothing, seventy-four."

"How many brothers and sisters do you have?"

"We started at fourteen," he said. "If he goes, we'll be down to eight. And they're all old now. I got a sister eighty-three, another eighty. Even the baby was born 1950. It'll be one after another now."

He thought about it.

"We had some fun together, me and Paulie." With a near smile, he smudged a thumb across his fingertips. "It's over before you know it."

He sat there with his hands hanging between his legs.

"He used to drive me around in his car," he said, gripping a wheel and letting it go. "What's left?"

Philly came into the locker room.

In a hushed voice he said "Is there a God, Lou?"

Lou jerked his head like *You believe this guy?*

Philly said "After that train accident the other day, Manny told me there's no God. So I came in here to ask you."

"He wants a theological consultation, Lou."

"*Ugats,*" Lou said.

•

"Remember this place?" I ask her.

White ornate building on Third Avenue, looks like a cake: Scheffel Hall. The gas lamps still in place.

"Yeah, used to be Fat Tuesday."

"Remember Les Paul used to play here every week?"

"That's where I met Johnny," she said.

"Who Johnny?"

"Johnny Thunders. He wanted me to manage him. Because I got him a show at the Marquee. I told him 'Johnny, I can't even manage my own life, how'm I gonna manage someone else?'"

"'Johnny, you don't need a manager, you need a keeper.'"

"He liked me because I yelled at him. He wanted an advance for the show. I even got him more money. I think they were getting eight thousand to play the Limelight, I got him ten at the Marquee. Then he demanded an advance. I said 'Johnny, we're not doing that. And if you're going to try and extort an advance out of me, let's call the whole thing off right now.' So he asked me to manage him."

"Where was the Marquee?"

"On the west side."

"I think I was at that show."

"I've still got all the posters for it and flyers somewhere . . ."

·

"Ladies and gentlemen. The next. Brooklyn-bound. L train. Will depart. In approximately. Six. Minutes."

·

PLAYTIME AT THE PALLADIUM . . . DANCETE-
RIA DALLIANCE . . . NO CAN TELL AT NO SE
NO . . . LIMELIGHT LIAISON!

·

To Tere: "Can you believe we've never said what this is? Is it because once you say those words, there's only one way for things to go? Is it because saying them triggers commitment as a gun triggers a bullet?

"The buyers have got the loan and they're approved by the board. They close in a week.

"For all the stress, there were a million things that could have gone wrong that didn't. Her husband could have made it tough but he didn't go after her retirement money or even grill her about me. She never pushed it by spending the night here, not that he knew about. It never got ugly between them. They didn't even fight over the place, since neither of them can afford it.

"End of the month, June will be packing up and moving down to Jane's, a few blocks away. I never thought it would happen, but here it is."

•

738 GREENWICH VILLAGE GARAGE 742

•

THE JUNE AND JANE SHOW

JANE: Thirty years, she didn't come here.

JUNE: Can you blame me? You didn't come here either!

MIKE: Why, what happened?

JANE: She found a bug in her salad.

JUNE: I didn't find him, he climbed out of it!

MIKE: What kind of a bug?

JANE: A cockaroach! Just strolling along—

JUNE: A live cockroach! And Mark Satlof—before I could say anything—picked up the bowl—

JANE: [*Laughter*]

JUNE: —picked up the bowl and ran away with it!

JANE: And then the waiter came, he was very apologetic—

JUNE: He said "Can I get you something else?"

JANE: "No, thank you." In that little voice. He said "Is there any way that I can make this up to you?" "No, thank you." Then out comes the manager. "Miss, anything on the menu! Anything at all!" "No, thank you." With that tone. Very polite.

JUNE: What would you have said? You'd have said "Fuck you, I'll never eat here again!"

JANE: "Miss, is there anything at all we can—" "No, thank you." Very proper, so it sends a chill down your spine.

•

Lou calls to say he picked up the magazines. A big stack this week: the usuals plus *Real Simple*, with fall checklist and decluttering ideas.

He says "I left you a package at the desk. I left you some prosciut'."

"You didn't have to do that, Lou."

"It's the Citterio. You know that one?"

"Sure, it's good."

"I left two packs of it."

"Why two? Won't you eat it?"

"It's the three-ounce pack, you make one sandwich."

"Thank you, Lou."

"Nice and pink. Because the dark red is too dry."

"I'll use it tonight."

"The pink is soft."

"Maybe I'll cut it up in the salad."

"You have to leave it out. I take it out of the fridge and let it get to room temperature, so it's got the full, y'know. I wait till the fat softens up—"

"Yeah, till it gets a little translucent."

"Riiiight, riiiight. Usually I have it with mozzarella, but I didn't have any mozzarella. So I left you a small roll of brie."

"Lou, it's great but it's too much. Thank you. I'll pick it up now. I'll be there in a minute."

"Oh, you're not home?"

"No, I'm walking from Chelsea Market. I went to buy squid."

"You already bought the squid?"

"Yeah. I'm gonna fry it with parsley and garlic."

"How much?"

"Ten dollars a pound."

"Ten dollars a pound! You kidding?"

"For the local, from Rhode Island. From Spain it's sixteen."

"My mother used to make it all the time, it was pennies. This was a peasant dish, it wasn't a fancy—"

"Well, this is cleaned and tenderized or whatever. And everything's fancy now, you know that."

"I used to go the Fulton Fish Market, they had it ten, fifteen cents a pound!"

"When, in 1948?"

"In 19 . . . 77. The summer of Son of Sam. Lou Salica had a stand there. He was a bantamweight champ. World champ. Ever heard of him?"

"No. Lou—?"

"Salica: S-A-L-I-C-A. Look him up. He weighed one eighteen. He was only about five five, he weighed one eighteen. Not then. By then he weighed probably one thirty-five, had a little pot belly. You couldn't meet a nicer guy. He used to sell the *galama* ten cents a pound, sometimes two pounds fifteen, if he was closing up."

•

The sky is grey and God is on the breeze.

•

Saturday afternoon straightening up the house, Van Morrison playing. Every few minutes I'm at the window. She went to see her friend Mo in Queens, so she's coming from the J. Quiet out there for a change. Just the crew by the bodega.

One time a guy from Ohio's staying with me, Mark, his first trip to New York. Woke up on his first morning, went down to smoke a cigarette on the step. The kids across the street, dealers, had their eye on him. Six in the morning, it's them and Mark. Finally they sent someone across.

The kid said "What are you doing here?"

Mark said "I'm staying with someone."

The kid said "This building? What's his name?"

"Mike."

The kid thought it over. He said "Short white guy with his hair pushed back?"

"Yeah."

"Okay."

When I moved back here from San Francisco, I was looking for a place. My friend Greg gave me three real estate agents. He said "Go to this one because they're Polish, maybe they find you something in Greenpoint. Go to this one because they're really great, I've dealt with them before. And go to this other one because they're Italian."

So I went to the first two, struck out.

Walk into the last place, there's a guy in a tracksuit reading the *Form*. "What can I do for ya?"

I said "I'm looking for a place in the neighborhood. But I can only spend a thousand dollars."

Looks me up and down.

Says "Alright, fill this out." Hands me a clipboard with an application—three, four pages. All this information, they want. And now he's behind me, as if he's looking out the window.

I write "Mike . . . DeCapite," he says "You don't have to go crazy, filling that whole thing out."

Then he says "Now. When can you move?"

I said "No rush. I can stay where I'm at for a month or two."

He says "No: when *can* you move, when *can* you move?"

I said "I can move tomorrow."

Says "Okay, I'll pick you up nine o'clock, I'll show you a place on the South Side in a building with an elevator won't be no garbage."

I walked out of there thinking *Aah, fuck! Why'd I ever get involved with this guy? There's no elevators in Williamsburg. Who knows what the hell he means by the South Side? Could be Sheepshead Bay!*

Next morning, 9:00, phone rings, he says "You ready?"

I said "Listen, I told you I can only spend a thousand a month."

He says "It's nine fifty-seven."

"Okay."

He says "You're Italian, right?"

"Yeah?"

He says "Me too. We never believe anything, even when it drops in our lap."

I don't know what my neighbors are cooking—some weekend Dominican dish: every Saturday the hall smells like boiling vinegar. In here, I've got eight lamb chops on a broiler pan with garlic and dill, a pot of kale on the stove with garlic and oil and two yams in the oven, and I keep looking out the window, waiting for June to turn the corner. Above the rooftops, the sky is bulging white like a grey balloon.

·

Saturday night in Brooklyn, all the barber shops are busy.

·

We get off the elevator at the Vermeer, coming home from a party. She's telling me she took ballet and tap when she was a kid. I unlock the door and kind of laugh inwardly at the picture of her doing tap, which becomes a stab of shame as I remember this is a real person. *Why not her?* I think as she goes into the dark apartment and hangs her coat in the closet.

·

Yogi Berra dies at 90. I didn't know he was still around. Lou says he met him. Lou was 10 years old. "He talked to everybody. And everybody the same, didn't matter: the owners, presidents, kids, guys on the street—because that's how he was." Berra noticed Lou watching warm-ups from the rail.

"You Italian?" he said.

"Yeah," Lou said. "Sicilian!"

"Me too," Berra said.

Lou said "You like lasagna?"

Berra said "I can't get enough of it!"

Nearly sixty years later, Lou pockets his wallet, closes up the small-valuables locker, and says: "I always wanted to meet him again, years later. See if he remembered this incident. I don't know why I said that, just came out of me. I always hoped I'd run into him again. Never did."

•

In the elevator she was bunching her hair in her fist and releasing it.

"Does my hair look *crazy?*"

"You look great."

"Because I didn't put anything in it this morning."

"You always look great. Forget about your hair."

She'd stopped listening.

"Does a tiger worry about how it looks? Do you ever think *This is a bad hair day for this tiger?* No, it's a tiger no matter—"

The bell went *ding* and she walked off the elevator.

•

Rainy wind announces the season. I stay in bed with her astral self until 7:30, then put on a jacket for the first time in months and make it to the subway, pointing my umbrella every which way like a shield, and zoom over to the Y in time to catch her umbrella coming along 14th Street . . .

After work, we come up the stairs at Essex into a wet mist. Fiddling with her umbrella, she gives me a look.

"I ask you if it's raining. 'A little,' you say. It's pissing with rain!"

I hold out my hand. Barely a drop.

•

With nowhere to land after work, we're always looking for something to do. Tonight it's a gallery on Orchard Street for a show of collages by Genesis P-Orridge. Once I was early for an opening at this same gallery and went for a walk to kill time. I walked past 56 Ludlow, which it occurred to me was the building where the Velvet Underground was born. I stopped on Orchard to look it up on my phone and a guy in a yarmulke sold me a suit. Walked up, said hi, and in fifteen minutes he went from "My father was in the store seventy years" to "Follow me, I'll give you a card" to "I'll take up the sleeves and see you Tuesday." Sammy, he's famous down there. A master salesman.

•

Halal carts, honey locusts, the sound of a small generator, a van backing up. Traffic moving forward. A few flags.

•

We follow Division past the bottom of Forsyth, through the wet lettuce boxes and broken pallets and under the Manhattan Bridge. Wherever you are in New York, you're at the heart of it. New York is holographic: every part contains the whole. Up Bowery to Bayard, where the puddles never dry and the garbage trucks never cease. I get a coffee with condensed milk and June gets a bun from a bakery where it's always three a.m. On a rainslick step I light a cigarette, she grabs me by the collar for a kiss. And we walk up Mulberry through Little Italy and what's left of the rained-out feast . . .

•

silvergrey sky pouring over the fountain's edge

•

At St. Mark's Books, I go up behind her to see what she's looking at. Of course it's the most interesting thing on the table. She's always drawn to the real thing. She has no taste for trash. Unlike me, she avoids it. Why consume something fake or toxic? She has a strong inclination toward self-improvement and none toward self-destruction or self-pity. Again, unlike me.

•

I'm buzzed if she uses the future tense. Any reassurance. It doesn't have to be "I'll never leave you." It can be "I'll see you in the morning." That's how uneasy I am. It could be "Let's go see that." If she leaves a bottle of conditioner at my house it's dizzying. Something anticipatory starts to sparkle in my chest, some chemical reaction. Fizzes up inside me.

•

Up Broadway, Strand is a night market. Verlaine's out by the dollar books, under the lights, with the moths. People don't look like that anymore in New York. Ascetic. Inter-dimensional. Not buying it. For me it's like there's Einstein and everybody's just passing him by on the sidewalk. Seeing him reminds me what's what. June too: he's her New York. Tonight someone's talking to him, he's half listening, with a cigarette in his mouth. "Don't ask me," he's saying. "I never met the guy."

At Fifth Avenue, June and I stop to look up at a water

tower charred into the sky. Then another goddamn good night at the L.

·

Looking down from the 22nd floor at the soft, seamed street below, a manhole cover embedded in the asphalt and the yellow lane stripes and white crosswalk nearly worn away.

·

Rooftop Manhattan, one in the morning. Her husband's at work. She said something I've never forgotten. We could see the flashes from the Empire State Building, the observation deck. She said she used to sit under the window sometimes watching those flashes up there in the night to feel less alone.

·

Back in that first September, I sat up in the corner of the couch smoking cigarettes. Scenes of her in various positions tumbled inside me like an X-Acto knife in a dryer. I waited for them to blunt their edge. For about a year. Bluewhite train smoke in a deep blue dusk.

·

I was at my locker getting dressed.

"Here, you're a big jazz fan," Lou said. "Read this."

I'm not a big jazz fan, but he once heard me mention Ornette Coleman, and because Lou tends to place the people he knows at the top of their respective fields, it pleases him to think of me as a "top jazz guy." I took the clipping, which came, as these pieces often did, from the *Italian-American Herald*, a paper in New Jersey. Lou's a subscriber.

He said "Jazz was invented by Italians."

"No kidding!"

"Ever hear of Nick LaRocca?"

"No."

"Cornet player from New Orleans. Wrote 'The Tiger Rag.' Sicilian. Ask him," he said, indicating Philly on his stool. Philly was pulling on a pair of pants of a color I can't quite name, somewhere between yellow and pink.

"Ask me what?" Philly said. "Ask me anything, I know everything."

"Ever hear of Nick LaRocca?" I said.

"No."

"He knows nothing," Lou said.

"Would a guy who knows nothing wear these pants?"

I said "You're claiming *jazz* now for the Italians?"

"At one time, there were five hundred thousand Italians in New Orleans."

"Sure," I said, "look at Cosimo Matassa."

"That's right!" he said. "He just died. How about Cosimo Matassa?" he asked Philly.

"I know Cosimo Matassa," Philly said. "He invented linguine."

•

THE JUNE AND JANE SHOW

We're walking home after a dish of pasta on Prince Street, Jane and June and I. With those two stopping at every window, it's only just faster than standing still. It feels like we're at least keeping ahead of the turning of the Earth, so we'll get home eventually.

We float into Washington Square in the dark, past the chess players . . .

JUNE: Parks are my favorite thing. Because everyone belongs. It's for everybody. Anybody could come here. Doesn't matter how cool you are, or uncool. Old, young. Anyone can come here and just sit. And not be bothered.

JANE: I always wanted to have a place at that end of the park, one of those townhouses.

MIKE: June has you growing up in one of those houses. She always points it out.

JANE [*laughing*]: No.

JUNE: Number seven.

JANE: No, I grew up on Ninth Street.

JUNE: You told me you grew up on the park.

JANE: You're confusing it. Maybe I told you Eleanor Roosevelt.

MIKE: Easy mistake. Just tonight I said we were having dinner with Eleanor Roosevelt.

JUNE: You make it up as you go along, don't you?

JANE: And Gertrude Stein lived there for a little while.

MIKE: Gertrude Stein was from Oakland.

JANE: She might be from Oakland but she and Alice lived here for a long time before they went to Paris.

MIKE: Really?

JANE: I'm not sure. That could be not true.

Now we're out of the park and waiting to cross.

JUNE: This is the part I don't understand. How can you just tell us things? If you don't know if they're true.

JANE: Nothing I tell you is true.

JUNE: How can you stand yourself?

JANE: Or ever will be.

JUNE: Knowing you lie, like a rug.

•

Wind—everything thrashing, swaying. Everything riding an ocean of wind.

•

Going over the Williamsburg Bridge on the J through the X-ing of girders and supports: the sky is orange and the river's mirror-blue and you know there'll be another winter.

•

A woman with a purple afro gets a running start, drops her board, and rolls past us . . .

•

I was standing in her kitchen about six in the afternoon, looking at the living room windows. The place was empty. The furniture, all the boxes. His stuff too. I slipped a roll of packing tape around my wrist, put a black marker in my pocket. My flip phone vibrated. To someone outside, the apartment would have been a box of late-in-the-day light just then.

M onday after work, rainy night, turned cold later, I
went to Bamonte's—I had a taste for braciole, pork
braciole. Dinner was mediocre but it killed the craving. And
then I was walking back on Devoe. The rain was stopped,
and at the end of the street there was a tree—backlit—just
standing there with its branches flung out against an orange
mist in a grand statement. For me alone. I was going straight
home because I had to work in the morning. Then I thought
*What the hell's become of you? Go smoke a bowl and make a
pot of coffee and write something and listen to music till three
in the morning. Pull an art book off the shelf. Have a fucking
thought! Who cares if you're tired at work tomorrow?*

Right away I wanted a cigarette. But forget it, I'm not
doing it. It's been a week.

Last time I quit I didn't have a smoke for a month, then
I went to see my folks, in Cleveland. After four hours I was
so tense I bought a pack at the gas station and drove around
the suburbs with the windows open, smoking and blasting a bunch of T. Rex songs. They still sounded great. And
that first cigarette was one of the great cigarettes. Big winds

were blowing the clouds behind the signs for Rite-Aid and Dunkin' Donuts, which are brighter than God. The profound eternal life-and-death teenage night was up there too. You never get older, not really. You never age inside.

While I was there my mother went in for an emergency triple bypass. That night I saw her in the recovery room. A person never looks quite so vulnerable as she does in a pale blue surgical cap. It's disturbing. Lying there with a tube down her throat and her tongue swollen to one side, she looked like she'd been hit by a truck. Like in a cartoon, with her tongue stuck out and *X*s for eyes. Her first words—I had to lean down to hear, she said "How's your father?"

Men go on dreaming and pitying themselves while women turn the crank that makes the world go around.

I stuck around to take care of my father. He'd had Parkinson's for a few years by then. I fixed his meals and saw to his medication. If there was nothing on TCM, I went to the library to get a movie for him.

I knew what to look for. Cagney, Bogie, Edward G. Robinson. I don't know how many times he asked me to look for *Dust Be My Destiny*, with John Garfield. Time and again I had to tell him the film was unavailable. And felt as if I was letting him down.

"See if they've got *Dust Be My Destiny*."

"They won't have it. That movie's never been rereleased."

"Oh, no?" he'd say. Newly disappointed. "See if they've got *Torrid Zone*."

"They won't have *Torrid Zone*. It's another one of those lost movies."

"See if they've got it."

"They don't."

"Why not? That's a damn good movie. James Cagney and Ann Sheridan."

"They don't have a special section of movies you saw at the Jennings Theater for a nickel when you were fourteen."

"Well, check anyway."

One of those first nights, after he was in bed, I snuck over to Walgreens. I wanted some disposable washcloths. You go in there out of the dark—Walgreens—it's an adjustment, a shift in consciousness. First of all, the place is lit for surgery. It takes a moment to adjust, you're like an animal that got in there and can't find its way out. You're confused by the lights and the things on the shelves—the sports drinks and counterfeit foods—99% of which have nothing to do with your life: the colossal plastic containers of cheese balls and the fabric shavers and Snuggies and neck pillows. They've got a *wearable* sleeping bag! How comfortable does a person have to be? Suburban life is stupefying. Two hundred kinds of toothpaste. Like everything else in this country, it's only the *illusion* of choice. Toothpaste or politician: a thousand choices, all of them mediocre. All toxic and differing only by the lies they tell: extra whitening, cavity protection, tartar control/Republican, Democrat, Independent. By that extra twist of mint. The only thing comparable in my life in New York is Bed Bath & Beyond. You go in there for razors and you come out a couple hours and $200 later with no memory of how you got there, or what else you were involved with in your life at that point—or your family or the town you grew up in, or your sexuality, or your name. You're starting from right now, with two big plastic bags. Back at Walgreens, the lights are buzzing, you go up and down these aisles: you feel really *alone* among the people who consume this stuff. And you get a sense of the predatory powers massed above you. Obviously if they're trying to sell you microwavable Beefy Mac & Cheese they mean you harm, right? And you're the only one there: it's like everyone else has been wiped out.

There's no one in the whole store, row after row—except for the row I'm looking for. Right now there's one guy, and it's Nicky Raven—later Nikki Raven in the eighties after he moved to LA—comparing the forty types of adult diapers. Probably back in town taking care of someone. And he's hypnotized by choice, like anyone would be. Beltless? Extra absorbency? With aloe? How long's he been floating around in here? I haven't thought about him in thirty years. At least thirty years. I was new on the scene when he was playing the bars with the last version of his band Ravens Laughter. He was mysterious because he'd opened for the Dolls and put out a single. Plus he was from an older generation—glam or shock metal. He was from a generation that still believed in stars and expected to get signed. He never really made the transition to punk, but he'd be at a show now and then, and he had an air about him. He was a rock star except for the fame. He left town way back when and faded into legend in LA, and now here he is in the fluorescent light with his one-thousandth black dye job and last faded pair of black snakeskin jeans and a serviceable pair of pointy children-of-the-night bondage shoes in the diaper aisle. Family gets you in the end. He's a little haggard, carrying more weight. Still kind of unapproachable. And he sees me and we acknowledge each other—he's trying to place me—we nod.

I woke up later my father was in the doorway, naked. Just his presence woke me, the eeriness of it. He glows in the dark. What's he want? He steps out from behind your ideas of him—he's in *his* life, not yours, and suddenly at the end of it, in this white body, his oldest companion. I jumped across the room and took his arm. "Pa, what are you doing?" I was naked too. So there we were. He looked at me like I could explain it. He was different in the night, part of a different realm. And his consciousness was more porous lately. He had vivid dreams. One night he was chased by a lion and woke up hollering. I was touched by how elemental the danger. Another night he cracked his head open on the dresser throwing himself out of bed to catch a fly ball.

"Pa, where you going?" I asked him, as he moved past me toward the couch and lifted the sheet. Maybe he was looking for my mother. I felt as though he was moving toward some ancient place where we all slept together, right after I was born, or where all families slept together for warmth and safety, in caves.

"Pa, you can't sleep here," I told him.

"I can't?" he said.

"You can, but this is where I'm sleeping. Ma's in the hospital. Don't you want to sleep in your own bed?"

"Where is that?"

"Come on," I said, and I walked him through the apartment, holding him by the arm as he took his determined compliant baby steps. "How'd you get here?" I asked him.

"Well," he said. "I just . . . followed along."

The next day was business as usual. There was nothing on TV, so I told him I was going to the library to get a movie to break up the afternoon.

"Anything you're in the mood for?"

"Gangsters," he said.

O ctober washed in with the rain. Now the clouds are tearing themselves open on the uplit Empire State Building like a scene from some 1930s dirigible-captain serial and she's through the door in a raincoat and short dress and tall black boots, with her purse and the mail and a brown shopping bag, crashing in on a wave of her own anticipation because I've been in a mood and she's carrying a bouquet of sunflowers, and she says "These are for you!"—a burst of yellow sunflowers in brown paper—but it's nothing compared to that smile, I mean just the biggest irresistible smile as she comes through the door with her nose wrinkled, laughing already at having this done for me, the excitement and deliciousness of it, the sheer luck of our being together right here and now.

•

"What news on the Rialto, Bubbie?"
   "D'ja see Jackie?"
   "Why, what's with Jackie?"

"He had the other knee, he's at Village Care."
"For how long?"
"Till tomorrow or Friday."
"I'll go tomorrow."

•

first leaf stains on pavement

•

One minute I'm walking home from school kicking through leaves with half a headache and sunlight prismatic in my eyebrows and the next, I'm driving my mother's car through a park with the sun at that same after-school angle after I've moved her into assisted living, gotten rid of her furniture and most of her clothes and sent the photo albums down the chute. Getting back to New York, I feel like I finished writing a novel: I just want to stare out the window. These are the days of endless afternoons. Banging from a construction site. The kind of days you'll remember forever and forget by tomorrow—these are the days. A steel ventilator in a blue sky.

•

REGISTERED

NO. 6240876

STATE OF NEW YORK

MOTOR VEHICLE

REPAIR SHOP

•

Subway doors open on two people under the stairs in a nest
of blankets. She's asleep, he's propped on an elbow, having a
smoke. Laundry draped on the enclosing rail.

•

Way back in that first autumn, with June living at Jane's and
a river between us, we still spent most of our nights apart and
snatched what time we could on the weekends. June carried
a lime-green canvas overnight bag, which is sitting above our
heads on a luggage rack on a dark October morning as we sail
out of the Lincoln Tunnel on a Trailways bus, Catskill-bound.

"I could live in Weehawken," I announce, looking out
the window.

"No."

"No?"

"What would you do there?"

"I'd . . . become active in Weehawken politics. I'd use the Fountain Motel—"

"Stop it."

"—as a place for accepting bribes and kickbacks on shady development deals."

"Would you be rich?"

"I'd be perceived as rich. But my ambitions and lifestyle would always outstrip my resources."

•

"D'ja go up and see Lester?"

"Yes, I went yesterday."

"I went, but he wasn't in his room. He look good?"

"He did. He's tired, but the surgery went well."

"He sounded good when I called. Who's picking him up?"

"I'm not sure. He'll be discharged Monday or Tuesday."

"I'll stop there tomorrow."

•

Woman with a broomstick yoke of recycling outside Duane Reade. Shirtless guy pushing a shopping cart lashed with bags of cans and bottles. A line of these prairie schooners in the parking lane.

·

"I went once, Tere. There's a brown awning on 11th Street, in the urn district, where everybody goes. Tony recommended a woman there and I made an appointment. I told her what was going on and she seemed to think it had something to do with my father's death, which didn't ring true for me.

"Also? By that point I hadn't had a cigarette in a week and I was feeling different anyway. So I didn't go back."

·

"Yeah, Mike: Lou. I got your message—Jeez, you got the thing this fast? I just dropped it off! I was gonna call you and tell you about it. But anyway: what it is basically—I received this from a doctor from Spain. If you notice, there's not one word in English on the whole thing, it's really from Spain. It's ah, it's basically it's made from ah—pigs that they only feed them acorns. It's the same acorn-fed pig that they get the Iberico ham—that famous ham? Now, the ham comes from the leg: this comes from the back. So—this is like a capocol'. You can make a sandwich with it, you can serve it like hors d'oeuvres, y'know, on a platter, before you eat. But I wasn't impressed with it! If you notice I opened it, because I wanted to try it, so I could tell him, and I made a sandwich with it, I cut some pieces off. It was kinda chewy! It wasn't tender. So I want you to eat it and tell me what you think of it. But it's uh . . . one of the finest uh— To me, it reminds me of capocol'! But capocol' is better than that. And uh, it's a fine product . . . Maybe I should just have it plain. And just chew it. I dunno, but in a sandwich? It didn't bite off! The whole piece pulled. So I wasn't crazy about it. Aright, so I hope you enjoy it: slice it up, have it with uh, y'know, with breadsticks or whatever, I dunno, make a sandwich with mustard—like that. Aright I hope you enjoy it: it's uh, it's like, it's a gourmet kind of a cold cut, y'know, it's a—*salumi*. Aright, I'll talk to you later."

•

We'd just smoked some hash. "Station to Station" came on. Gradually, it came on. You know, the steam, the platform. We became very involved with the train sound at the beginning. It went on forever. From Berlin to Cologne, it went on. And then the guitar, wailing.

"How great is that?" I said.

"Wow."

"See?"

"See what?"

"Have you ever heard this?"

"It's David Bowie, 'Thin White Duke.'"

That cracked me up. Because I knew it wasn't her thing.

But she could pull this silly phrase from forty years' deep storage, even though she didn't care about Bowie. There was something about our age or parallel history.

I said "What's not to like about this?"

"I never understood David Bowie, it's like science fiction."

I keeled over to one side laughing.

"What's not to understand about this? Listen to the sound of that. That's all you gotta know."

But now Bowie came on, intoning. Doing his Nazi vampire cokehead bit.

"I want to know what's going *on*, Michael. I want to know what's happening."

I was doubled over. I couldn't breathe. She meant *What does he want?* You know. *What's he want from me?* She's immune to pretension. She wants music that's unequivocal. Music that's on the make. I fell through a wormhole of adoration and laughter.

A Suicide song came on. June said "He asked for my number once, Alan Vega. I was so embarrassed."

"Why embarrassed?"

"I was young then. I didn't—speak up for myself. I didn't have any moxie yet."

I had a revelation. There was nowhere else I wanted to be. Including alone. With June I was *where I wanted to be.* It registered like the sound of a gong. I never suspected this was a possibility. Always, in the past, whoever I was with, I secretly wished I were elsewhere. Even if it was off by myself, typing and drinking or whatever. I just thought that's how it is. Who knew it could be this way?

"I'm really *high*," she said.

I thought about that.

Then I said: "I feel like *high* is not the right word for this."

"What?"

"I feel like *high* is not the right word for this. It sounds like you're high above where you usually are. You know what I mean? Separate from it. But this is not separate from who I am, this is who I am. This stuff brings me *back* to who I am. Like this is who I'm supposed to be. Like this is who I'd always be if I were paying attention."

"What else?" she said.

Back down the wormhole I went.

"What else, honey?"

We'd been there for another hour when the phone rang. It was her mother.

When she hung up, our attention went back to the music.

Half an hour later, she said "My mother had a comment for everything. Then she asked me what we were doing and

I said 'Listening to records.'" June passed a hand in front of her face: "Nothing! Total silence. She had nothing to say to that. Probably thought *How crazy is that?*"

"'We're burning the coffee table,'" I said.

Our laughter increased.

"You should tell her something different every time she calls."

She was waving me away, laughing.

"'Us? We're taking the stuffing out of the pillows.'"

She kept waving me to stop.

"'We're turning the vases over.'"

Laura Nyro came up on shuffle.

We listened.

I said "She seems like the kind of person people say 'She's very talented!'"

She started laughing.

"Right?" I said. "Like she's hearing that her whole life. 'She's very talented!'"

Another Laura Nyro song came on. She seemed to be playing the chord changes as they arrived in her head.

After a while it was like we had a situation on our hands.

"I put this record on every couple of years," I said. "But after about fifteen minutes I feel like *I'm* losing my mind or *she* is, so one of us has to go."

This time, it was me. We left the apartment. Laura Nyro drove us out. I was locking the door behind us. The song was still playing. Laura Nyro was singing her heart out.

I said "That to me is the sound of neurosis."

She nodded.

I said "In fact, if I had to choose one word to describe what Laura Nyro sounds like, that would be the word: *neurosis.*"

"Yeah, she's crazy," June said easily.

I stopped to look at her.

"Simply put, yes."

We started laughing.

We were laughing uncontrollably.

We stopped.

"Michael," she said, putting a period on it.

•

"It's been two weeks now, Tere. Turns out I didn't need therapy. I just needed to quit smoking. Soon as I quit, I lost all that agita, tsuris, fear and trembling. Looked around for it, it wasn't there.

"Which is not why I quit—I've tried a million times to quit smoking, but maybe I'm finally able to do it because if I'm asking someone to stick around and have a future with me, I have to do what I can to be there.

"I still see those clips of her with other guys, but I don't sit and watch them on repeat. I think the same thoughts. But without cigarettes I can't make an activity out of thinking them. I feel what I feel, I don't have to act it out, as well. Without a prop for my anxiety, I don't turn it into an opera.

"It's hard to make more of anything than it is.

"Which I have to admit is the one thing I miss. Without alcohol and now without cigarettes, I have no way anymore to settle into a moment or to hang on to it, I have to let it pass. Life just keeps on happening."

•

One night after work I stood at the corner of 50th and Sixth looking at the Radio City sign on a night without June. Maybe she was working or maybe it was that first autumn, after she sold her place and moved over to Jane's. Anyway, the list of what there was to do without her ran through my fingers like the end of a film. I wandered down to Grand Central, which inescapably stands for the world. Even has its own sky. The first time I moved to New York I got off the train here with a manual typewriter and bag of books. Including a dictionary! I tried to watch myself through that kid's eyes as I moved with the crowd, but it didn't give me a lift, and neither did the boards for the Harlem Line,

Hudson Line, and New Haven Line, or the skylit catwalks, or the seagreen zodiac firmament. You can't always get it up, imaginationwise. So I got on the train to 14th. Some mariachis came on the L and played for two stops before passing the hat. I walked up Marcy and let myself into the apartment and didn't bother turning on a light, just climbed into bed. But the bed without her was zero comfort. Like sleeping at a bus stop.

·

And there she is in a white bathrobe with her hair in clips, busy at whatever she does in the kitchen in the morning. Putting the dishes away, setting up the coffee. Whatever it is, she's got a whole system going on. Just under my sternum, a right whale breaches.

·

I lie awake in the precancerous dark listening to the sound of space at the windows. A *field* of sound: the base sound of the city, the humming of the world's dynamo. An active sound of nothing in particular. I get up to take a leak.

"What's happening?" she says, from sleep. "Everything okay?"

●

Sunday evening at Elephant & Castle, a woman doing the *Times* crossword with a glass of wine, a salad, and a half order of shoestring fries.

●

It was only about six in the morning, June was at the table reading something online. She'd been getting hot flashes. Feeling other changes. She was reading for a long time. Then she closed out and shut the computer down. She sat there looking out the window.

Finally she said "I'm gonna look older." She turned and looked at me, to gauge my understanding of that.

I nodded.

It was just getting light, and there was a new crane on the skyline.

●

She put her head on my chest, I put my face in her hair, and she slept while we fell through space.

●

•

THE JUNE AND JANE SHOW

JUNE: Jane, what kind of cake do you have at home?

JANE: Donuts.

JUNE: Tell me what kind of cake.

JANE: Jelly donuts. Chocolate glazed—

JUNE: What kind of cake?

JANE: It's a banana cake with nuts—

JUNE: No I don't like it.

JANE: Sort of a cashew cream—

JUNE: No I don't *like* it.

JANE: With a hint of hazelnut—

JUNE: That's my least favorite nut!

JANE: And a layer of ground filbert.

JUNE: You are the most annoying person.

MIKE: A nice Entenmann's.

JANE: With a cinnamon swirl.

JUNE: Stop speaking.

JANE: Y'know, when I was growing up—and I won't tell
you what era that was—there was not one Jew, anywhere, who didn't mention a coffee ring at least once at
some point during the day. Not one. You never went a

day without picking up a coffee ring or saying "Pick me up a coffee ring." And it was always delicious.

•

When Lou and Bernard are finished with the crossword—standing, Bernard with a length of dental floss hanging out of his mouth—Lou comes to the mirror near me to put on his sunblock.

"Lou, I made the best dinner last night. And it was so easy."

"What'd you do?"

"I softened garlic in oil with a little red pepper. I opened a can of beans."

"The cec'?"

"I used great northern. Tore up a head of escarole. Oregano, a little lemon. And I tossed it with pasta. I used the ditali you gave me."

"Did the beans go inside?" he wants to know. He pokes a finger.

"No, the ditali's too small."

"Oh, if you use the lentils they go inside."

"Tonight I'll make lentils."

"*Le lenticchie!*" he cries.

"I make 'em with broken-up linguine. More like a soup."

"*In brodo.* You can make it two ways," he says, moving in. "*In brodo*—wet, loose." He demonstrates, rolling his shoulders. With a towel around his neck, like my corner-man. "More like a soup. Or—" He closes up, goes into a crouch. "*Asciutta*—dry, tight. You tighten it up."

I slam my locker and snap the lock.

"Tighten it up," he's saying. "Tighten it up."

•

Three mornings in a row I played *Goats Head Soup*. On the third, June said "Are you on shuffle or you're listening to a record?"

"This is *Goats Head Soup*. Why?"

"This was my only—I played this record over and over. As soon as I got home from school, I'd go in my room and *blast* this record until my father got home. Because that was the only time I could do it. The whole house would shake. I got home at three thirty, and I had until five thirty."

"You had a record player in your room?"

"Yeah. I had my room, and I was very self-contained. The only time I had to go out of there was to the bathroom."

"But this couldn't have been your only record."

"When did they put it out?"

"Seventy-three."

"What did they make, one record every year?"

"Yeah."

"It was probably the only Rolling Stones record I had.

No. Because I had the *Majestic*—" She tipped an imaginary lenticular jacket back and forth. "But that one was more trippy or something, this is the one I played over and over. And I used to dance around my room singing 'Fuck a star, fuck a star!' It was very exciting."

•

A white '65 T-bird swung out in front of me in traffic. And knowing its name reminded me that some of the pleasure of being alive is in knowledge and memory and the reassurance that your consciousness is a continuum, and therefore so are you.

•

a sudden thrill of wind

•

We were walking along Gramercy Park. On the southeast corner there's a dark brick fortress, the kind of place where, before I met June, I used to fantasize I'd wind up rich, friendless, and safe from time.

Later I look it up online. Apartment 8AR is for sale. It's $3.5 million.

"The listing says James Cagney lived in the building. And Margaret Hamilton, the Wicked Witch. Maintenance is six grand a month."

"Forget it," June says. "We can't even afford the maintenance, let alone the apartment."

"Three bedrooms, two baths."

"It's perfect," she says. "Jeff could come and stay—"

Twice a year my friend Jeff came to visit from California and I gave him my place in Brooklyn.

"Jeff would have to live with us. And pay half the maintenance. And come up with the three million."

•

The darkness breathes traffic.

•

I was looking at a Google map of the world. June brought me a coffee.

"Maybe we should go to Svalbard," I said.

"I would go there."

"Do you know where it is?"

"No."

This is one of her signal qualities: she's game. She's in. I clicked minus minus minus and the place receded into the pale blue of the Barents Sea and then the Arctic Ocean.

"Is there a place I could name that you wouldn't want to go?"

"Florida," she said.

•

I go to sleep now and wake up with dread.

•

While the sky emptied and the city settled into night, I waited on the traffic island at Seventh Avenue and Christopher. By the newsstand. I texted her what side of the street I was on. And pictured her coming up the subway stairs and marching straight in the wrong direction. That's June: walk like you know right where you're going. Even when you don't. I was there half an hour while time flowed around me. Guy with headphones walked by eating a taco from a wrapper, reading a book. Presently, I was able to hear through to the city's quiet. Just the thump of the taxis on Seventh Avenue like wind. The living silence of a meadow at night. I waited so long I felt as if I owned that triangle. A newsstand, a mailbox to lean on. *Village Cigars*, white on red.

•

the blinking red/blue faces of people at café tables as a fire truck goes by

•

Thursday midnight L platform. A rat goes momentarily along the wall, the color of the track bed, which seems to be one oil-soot substance like the black compressed fallout of time. She's got a thing about rats. Last night on Marcy Avenue one ran across our path and she said "Oh, that's boring," and veered away. Greasy white tiles, water dripping. When I dropped her off at Jane's she said "Don't talk to anyone." Darkness down the tunnel. I feel a little drunk with her swimming in my eyes, buzzing in my ears.

•

Out the window, empty morning: a pop-up neighborhood on a grey background.

In here, a vase of red roses, breadcrumbs on a red tablecloth from our dinner last night. The sight of your A-shirt puts an ache in me. A pen you left behind.

I get an email there's something at the desk. Turns out it's a shopping bag with five pounds of pasta from Lou. Rigatoni, ziti, penne, butterflies, mezzi gomiti. Imported, nice stuff. Next day I see him on the track.

"What's doin'?" he says. He drops the *Post* on his stack and we go around.

"Thank you for the pasta. I've got it piled on the counter, like treasure."

He says "When you cook that pasta—I don't know how much you make, but say you normally make twenty rigatoni."

"I usually figure a quarter pound each person."

"I never weigh it, but okay. You're making a quarter pound of rigatoni: you make *half* of that, and you throw in the same amount of ziti or penne. Throw 'em in together, don't worry about what it says on the bag. Throw 'em in together, don't worry, they'll get done."

"Okay." There's no way I'm doing this.

"When it's in the water—because it's boiling violently!— somehow, the ziti goes *inside* the rigatoni, some of it. It goes inside there. This way, you get two. It's chewy! Two pastas at once, with the sauce in there. Delicious!"

•

She was putting away the dishes and she came out of the kitchen in a white cotton shift, looking like an Italian movie star.

•

THE JUNE AND JANE SHOW

In a crosstown taxi . . .

JUNE: I'm gonna hit you.
JANE: I'm gonna—you're not even gonna see me comin', I'll be so—
JUNE: Vicious. *Short*, and vicious.

•

Today I had my iPod on my desk at work because I had it from the gym. The women I work with clustered around. They had some laughs about it while I worked.

"Becca thought it was a medical device!" I tell June. "Little do they know I've also got a thousand CDs and a shelf of records. And a big box of cassettes. TDK C90s, some of them with handwritten cards. In blue Bic, over bumpy dried correction fluid. Some of them faded from being in the car."

June says "I don't know when the world changed."

"Because it happens gradually. Step by step, you go from the inside to the outside. Life is a process of being gently shown the door."

•

Go to the gym every day and you wind up with a web of tacit relationships: people you like at a distance but never talk to. People you feel are simpatico for some reason. The bony old man who, in his watchful nonjudgment, reminded me of my father and always looked at me with a twinkle of recognition. We nodded to each other every morning until one day I noticed he hadn't been there in a while, and he never was again. A tall woman with a ponytail who's quit coloring her hair. Sam and Deborah, who live at the Vermeer, and whose evident rightness as a couple draws you toward them. A brawny woman with a different kind of attention on her face, looks like a nun who slipped out of her habit to work out with the dumbbells every morning. Willie, a beanpole in his eighties, who comes from a shelter uptown and spends his day here doing yoga and stretching. I'm not sure I've ever heard him utter anything but an encouraging word. Father Joe—95 if he's a day—he landed at Normandy!—wiry, bandy-legged, smiling—with long white hair and that true Catholic homing instinct that sees the best in people and seems aware of but unaffected by the ugliness in the world. He's almost beyond gender he's so pure. It's a pleasure to see him in the morning. Seeing him shifts you, like music.

And of course there are people you dislike with never a word exchanged between you. But the worst aren't the ones you'd expect. It's not the guy in a permanent rage because four years ago someone got to a machine before him, and who sprays and wipes everything down before using it, including his own basketball, which he carries in a duffel bag. (People here fall into two categories: those who wipe down the machines after using them and those who wipe them down before.) It's not the freak who wants to know if you're a Jew and compulsively jams the trash barrel up against your locker, even while you're there, and with whom you've twice come right up to blows.

No, the ones who really get to you are the ones who remind you of yourself. It's a schmuck like Skeezix, who spends his nights at theater and the movies and hustles in here every morning to disgorge his impressions and opinions on everyone. Toddles into the cardio room with an armload of newspapers and a jumbo water bottle and leans on the back of some woman's bike, giving her the benefit of his insights, like a high school English teacher, and relieving his back of the weight of his belly. She cuts her workout short, he moves to another woman. When that one splits, he lugs himself after David Rothenberg, on the track. He goes all around the place interfering with people's workouts. A predatory bore. Gets on a recumbent bike, opens the *Times* like a map, and spends the next half hour listing toward his neighbor, informing him and forgetting to pedal. And he's one of those guys has to get up close to make a point. He's educating Angel, the locker room attendant, leaning over the towels. He's got a guy pinned down at the sinks, dissecting a musical made in 1958. Follows Tim into the shower reciting baseball stats. He's talking through a toilet door.

He's probably driven his wife insane. I'm sure this is how June sees me. Just today she's trying to shave her legs and I'm in there recounting one of my frequent revelations about some song recorded fifty years ago, talking to her through the steam. She doesn't seem to be listening.

I ask her: "Am I getting on your nerves?"

She says "You're very chatty this morning."

Today he's on a StairMaster, Skeezix, with the paper. Just reading the Arts section up there, not moving. A girl steps off a machine, sees a friend. So they're catching up. Interrupting his reading. Skeezix is craning around so they'll know his displeasure. He's pissed they haven't given him a chance to weigh in. Finally he speaks up—tells them to take it someplace else. They move away. And now he's bitching about them—across two people on stair machines—to a woman at the end of the row. I can hear him through my headphones.

•

I walk into Wu Liang Ye after work on a rainy Thursday night and there she is down the room, smiling at me, showing not a trace of the long workday. Waving. Me, I work an extra half hour I act like I'm coming off a 36-hour shift in an army field hospital. She left the house at seven this morning and there she is—lit up—at a two-top, out of the rain.

I kiss her and sit down, she says "You are so. Smart. To think of coming here. You're the smartest man I know."

•

Saturday afternoon, reading on the bed. My attention wanders from the page to the window outside ours, the water-tower skylines superimposed in rising ranks— dozens of water towers, and all the intricacies of a cityscape lit by the sun: facades, arched windows, cornices, cranes, scaffolding—row on row of these in the placid light, every detail registered on the glass plate. A world without mass, without time, without sound, dreaming itself all day in the glass. With a frame around it. One puff of rising steam.

•

On an overcast Sunday morning she went down on me and coaxed it all out of me, every thought in my head, all of the past. Left me staring at the ceiling, blank.

•

Yesterday I had one of those mornings your pants are too long and your hair's not right and you hate your shirt and you look like an old balding eunuch in the train window, just completely off your step, and I get to the gym I keep dropping things and my headphones get snagged and yanked halfway off my head until I'm in a fury. And then I realize: thirty days since I had a cigarette. The last three times I tried to quit I went a month and then lit up under stress. So that's what this is about. Fear of commitment. Trying to get myself wound up so I light a cigarette. Because if I cross the one-month threshold, I have no excuses.

If you can get through *not smoking* without smoking, what excuse do you have?

Anyway, nothing to see here. Let's keep it moving.

•

I miss you tonight, after the rain, near midnight, and truck-booms and traffic-wash from the BQE, and a chill from under the window, and October, and you recent to this bed.

•

We're walking to buy groceries when I'm stopped by some ginkgos on 13th. Leaves utterly yellow, sky utter blue. It stops me inside. And that effect reminds me it's me in there, and not some impostor. At the same time, this sight goes so deep, so far back, that am I even me anymore, at that point? June's half a block away before she notices I'm not there. I'm still here, staring up at the leaves and sky. Every year, I run up against this and my inability to describe it. This juxtaposition—yellow on blue—is one of the absolutes, where words run out. Beyond meaning. There are others in other seasons. In autumn, it's this.

•

DAY ON CORSA & CO
IMPORT RS
TEAS AND COFFEES

•

Clear cold October morning we're reading in bed when I remember Lou's magazines. Pull on some clothes and make it downstairs with his *People* and *Entertainment Weekly*, plus *Coastal Living*, with holiday decorating tips, and *Food & Wine*. A maintenance guy is hosing off the sidewalk. Here comes Lou with his plastic handle bag. "You didn't have to make a special trip!" he scolds. Reaches in the bag, pushing aside gym shoes, coupons, newspapers—"This is for June"—frees up a bottle in a bag from a hardware store. A Montepulciano.

"Oh. Very nice."

"I also got a bottle of Sangiovese. Very good. It's the number-one grape in Itly. The blood of Jove. It's the oldest grape. Goes back to the Romans, this grape."

"This one's enough, Lou. She'll like this."

"Does she like red wine?"

"She likes this one."

"She drinks white wine? What does she like?"

"No, no, this is good."

"Pinot grigio?"

"Please. I don't want you to buy it."

"Nah, nah, I just like to know what people like."

"She likes Sancerre."

"Oh, dry, crispy. Like a cheaper Meursault."

I wonder if he can smell pussy on my face and move

myself downwind. We stand outside the building talking about the prices of things and what we've eaten this week.

"I went to Joe's," I tell him. "Joe's of Avenue U, in Gravesend. Anyway, I thought of you: they had *vastedda* on the menu."

"They still got the *vastedda*? What else they got?"

"Well, they've got that pasta with sardines—"

"Oh, with the *finocch'*—"

"That's right, and raisins—"

"And the *pignole*. That's a Sicilian dish."

"Right. It's a Sicilian place."

Jim comes across the street. I've met him, he runs numbers out of the Donut Pub, but Lou reintroduces me as a top guy, one who never wears a hat, even in the coldest weather. Lou's wearing a watch cap and Jim's got a tweed newsboy. Jim says "What about Aldo? He never wears a hat." And they start telling me about Aldo, who likes to walk.

"Remember he walked to Coney Island?"

"He walked to Yonkers one time!" Lou said.

"I was on a bus on Eighty-Sixth Street, I looked out and there he was! Though that's nothing for Aldo."

"Aright, let me go," Lou said. He had to get on with his errands.

•

Rain here all day. Wet leaves on parked cars and in the gutter, leaf stains on the sidewalk. Cooking soup.

•

And every night the sirens. What more do you need to know?

S tanding on the corner of 34th and Lex, after Samuelson, waiting to cross. Grey November, a nothing day.
One of those motionless days outside of time. A few years
ago June got me started with these doctor visits. Before that
I never in my life went to a physical that wasn't for a job. In
the first three months she got me set up with a GP, a dentist,
an eye doctor, and a Park Avenue dermatologist who went
over me with a wand. At some point you go from watching for danger from outside to expecting it from within.
Samuelson dismissed me with an all-clear. Few years ago,
that wouldn't have been a big deal. But crossing Lexington,
I'm thinking *More time with June.*

•

"D'jear Willie's sick?"

"Yeah, I haven't seen him here."

"Yeah, I think it flared up again, the c-ncer. I don't think
we'll see him back here."

"Where's he at?"

"Jacobi, in the Bronx. A few of us are going up to see him this week."

"Let me know."

•

Warm November morning. A puddle reflecting sky and a yellow honey locust, a maintenance man hosing down the sidewalk. Yellow leaflets plastered here and there. Without the cold, when you don't have to fight your environment, you can expand and breathe. Someday there'll be no more of these mild mornings that take you back fifty years: the strong breeze, wet sidewalks. This is what you lose.

•

"Is she a good dancer?"

"Whadaya mean is she a good dancer?"

"Well . . . How does she *dance*?"

While Jeff's in town from Stinson Beach, we go to see the Waldos at Bowery Electric, Walter Lure's band. The place is packed—it's backed up to the door, but Jeff and I follow Jane and June as they cut through the crowd, a couple of old pros, to the edge of the stage. Back in the nineties, June was with Walter's younger brother, Richie, so she's a friend of the family. Walter sees them and dedicates a song to them, "Love That Kills," June's favorite. A ripple goes through her coat—this is where she lives, this New York roar that gives no ground and acknowledges nothing outside itself. Basically they're a more shambolic Heartbreakers. But Walter had a hand in those songs, so they sound about the same. And the sight of him with his bowler hat, tiger jacket, tie askew, and fuck-it attitude cheers you up—it's like seeing Bugs Bunny. They sound great—you want to throw all your cards in the air. *"Well you can CRY CRY CRY if you WANT TO"*—she and Jane are singing along, doing their dance, perfect for crowded clubs and other tight spaces. I call it the Canarsie. Raise one hand above the crowd, pointing at the music on the beat, then waving it side to side, while thinking of something else, maybe a bag you saw earlier . . .

●

We're driving home on the Belt Parkway at night, flying past the Verrazzano. I'm at the wheel, Jane's asleep in front.

In back, Jeff says "Nice, getting out here." By way of thanking us for taking him out in the car.

June's back there too. "See something different," she agrees.

Just three words, but in them I hear my Italian aunts—women with a direct connection to life and death—and I spiral through the dark considering her Brooklyn-bred empathy, her fundamental understanding of what a person needs, and the simplicity of her expectations, with the shadows coming at me out of the road.

•

The radiators clank, and hiss, and bang, and hiss.

•

After three days of media hysteria over the coming blizzard, after they pronounced it historic in advance and called it the blizzard of the century, after all the canceled flights and closed airports and chains on the bus tires, after the supermarkets sold out of bread including the honey-nut whole-grain English muffins and toaster-ready corn cakes and Portuguese festival spelt loaf, and after the bodegas sold out of bottled water including every last bottle with a label printed in Cyrillic, you know what happened? It snowed. Yes, on Saturday night it snowed, and Sunday we walked up Fifth Avenue through the slush moats at every curb, and I wound up in a boyfriend chair at Lord & Taylor.

•

White-topped water towers on a white sky. The snow is whiter by the minute, in contrast to the sky. There's no such thing as time, and the world is yours. Snow white on grey sky.

·

I missed her before dawn with the radiators coming on.

·

I'm so happy I'll turn to steam. Evanesce.

·

Early morning still dark I'm in the kitchen trying not to make any noise. In the other room, her first words are "Michael Michael Michael."

·

To Tere: "Six months, we're doing great. All I want to do is follow her from room to room. We're thinking of having an operation to turn ourselves into Siamese twins, sharing one of the minor organs. Or getting a pair of four-legged pants."

·

green Brussels-sprout leaves in a white sink

·

Lou calls, he's got a gift card for a juice place called Liquite-
ria. It came to him by way of the shadow economy of favors,
barter, and regifting in which he participates. In this case,
his buddy did some work for the owner of the place and the
owner couldn't pay so he gave the guy four $50 gift cards
and the guy gave one to Lou in payment or trade or tribute.
So Lou wants to take me there for a juice.

We're walking over, he tells me he found another wallet. Lou's in bed by 7:30, so he's up before the birds. Two
thirty, 3:00 he's walking the streets. Who knows why? But
he finds wallets. Not just once or twice: he's a finder of lost
wallets. He found one a few weeks ago with $230 and spent
a whole day tracking a woman to the Lower East Side, waiting outside till someone let him into the building, leaving
a note in her door, going back out to meet her in front of
Best Buy on Union Square to give it back. Now another one.
No money, just a card case with a driver's license and credit
cards, ATM. This guy's on 15th Street.

Lou called him and said "I'll meet you at Fifteenth and

Seventh, the southwest corner, at quarter to twelve. How will I know you?"

Guy said "I'll be wearing a pair of red jogging pants."

To me, Lou says "I figure he's gonna be anxious to get this, he'll be early, maybe twenty to twelve. So I leave the house eleven thirty, it's a five-minute walk because I stop at the deli, I get there eleven thirty-five. He's not there, I go into Sabon, the soap store—"

"Sabon? What for?"

"To get warm. It's cold out here! Plus you use the scrub and the hand cream."

"Okay."

"So eleven forty, he's not there. I see Jim across the street, I go across to talk to him. You remember I introduced you? Hangs around the Donut Pub."

"I remember."

"So I'm talking to him, now it's quarter to twelve, the guy's still not there. What a banana! Here I got his American Express, his driver's license, all his other cards. Can you believe this guy? Twelve o'clock he shows up—I can see him coming. So I let him wait, I finished talking to Jim and then I went over. The worst thing is dealing with people."

•

We've lost the Chrysler Building. One day there's a crane. A year later there's a black tower, all glass, like a strip of black redaction tape in the sky. Part of the proliferation of redactions that are canceling out the skyline of old water-tower New York. Not to mention Hudson Yards, which is like a Death Star landed on the west side. Jane says "Pretty soon it's gonna look like Dubai."

Not long ago we were driving back to the city and for the first time, I didn't recognize the skyline.

•

I sat in this room as it got dark. I didn't pick up a book or a magazine. Didn't get dinner started. Just sat on the couch, looking out the window. The sun had got below the cloud ceiling and chosen the Empire State and Chrysler Buildings and a band of apartment buildings, which stood in a dark blue sky transmitting now a burning auspicious gold, now vermilion. At 5:00 the lights at the top of the Chrysler Building started in quick increments like the opening of a fan, and soon the others, only just now red, had given up the ghost, gone dull, and left me with the feeling of a drug wearing off, returning me to my senses and time's flow, and it was just another night.

•

I zoned out, and was just about to reenter my life through a pinpoint portal, but I didn't know where I was coming into it. I mean—at what point? During what era? What skirmish or engagement? What was I coming back to? And where?

I was so relieved it was here with you!

•

Cathode-grey sky. The dead brown leaves went red with the taillights of a parking car.

•

She came down the subway stairs with her customary caution, and then she was laughing on the platform. Always gets me, that laugh. On the platform, I was watching the something-else in her silvergreen eyes—something not personal—a joy that was beyond her—and she was so alive I felt I was seeing her in the moment of her death. And I ached that this was her portion. That she should ever die. Not that I should lose her but that *life* should lose her. I mean I understand that rules are rules, I get it, I get it, but *everyone* has to die?—no exceptions?

•

Ahead of me on the sidewalk there's a guy with a shock of orange hair and a long black coat—an Egon Schiele figure come to life—pulling an aluminum walker—contorted—dragging it—*lunging* one step at a time—heroic!—along 14th Street in the morning rush.

•

L MANHATTAN 4 MIN.
L MANHATTAN 8 MIN.

A rainy night, on my way to her. It's always exciting, it's never enough, and it'll never end.

•

Lou and Philly are sitting in the lounge area with the whole day ahead of them.

Philly's saying "They didn't have a table for me in front, so they sat me in the TV room. But I made them turn off the TV. I told them 'I can't eat with a TV on.'"

"What place you talking about?" I ask him.

"Capucine's," he says. "It's an Italian restaurant for Irish people."

"I walked past a place on MacDougal Street last night," I tell him. "Little place three steps down. Said it's there since 1918."

"Monte's," they say in unison.

Philly says "They threw me out of there one night for wearing a hat. It used to be there were restaurants you couldn't wear a hat."

"There used to be a guy there," Lou says, leaning forward and lowering his voice, "Jewish guy, so tall he had to bend over to go in the kitchen. Herb. Nice guy."

"I remember," Philly says.

"He was there thirty years. You know how he got there?"

"How?"

"They needed a guy one night, they were short one guy. So they called up the agency, Martini, used to send guys to all the restaurants downtown. Waiters, short-order cooks. There was a guy looked like Spencer Tracy, he was a salad man. That's all he did, salads. He was an *artist*. He'd put designs on them, everything. They used to ask for him special, 'Send that guy.' They always wanted him to stay, but he didn't want a steady job."

"'Cause he drank, or whatever."

"Right, right. He lived in an SRO, ten dollars a night, on Broadway in the twenties, there used to be a lot of 'em. Anyway, this Herb—this is going back in the seventies now. They said 'Send over a guy for one night.' So they sent Herb. He was there for the next thirty years."

•

B&J FABRICS   B&J FABRICS
BEAUTIFUL FABRICS SINCE 1940
OPEN TO THE PUBLIC 2ND FLOOR

•

Our pal Clinton was in from London, we were talking on the couch. He brought up the subject of a man in England who was in the news because he turned 108 years old and got a letter from the queen. He's been getting them every year since he turned a hundred and he says they're piling up, these letters—enough's enough.

So we're laughing about that when June speaks up to say she once saw an item in the paper about a man in Florida who was about to have his hundredth birthday—they were encouraging people to write to him because he didn't have anyone left—and she sent him a card!

While I'm cracking up with this, Clinton says to June "See? You do something nice and *that* is what you get!" and she shrinks back down in her chair with an uncertain smile like she can't tell if she's being with or laughed at.

She says "I wanted him to get a birthday card from New York City."

"When was this?" I ask her.

"Long time ago," she says.

"Like when?" Figuring this is forever, right? Because

we're together ten years at this point, and she never mentioned it.

"At least a year ago, maybe two years."

"A year! You mean this happened recently? You didn't tell me about this!"

Now she's up and pretending to check her phone.

I said "So you went out and bought a card and addressed it to this man in Florida?"

She still thinks we're laughing at her, but I'm laughing because she's too good to be true.

"What'd you say, in the card? What'd you tell him?"

"I told him 'Way to go!'"

•

brown curls of onion skin in a white sink

•

"What time is it?"

She opened her eyes and checked. "Twenty-one twenty-eight."

"Almost nine thirty. Pretty soon we'll be going to bed at eight o'clock. Like the old Italians. Like Lou."

"What's wrong with that?" she said, eyes closed.

"It's okay for you because you're a woman."

"Don't lump me in with all other women," she said, turning over.

"I've never met a woman who didn't like to sleep."

"What do you like?" she said into the pillow.

"I like to be awake."

She said nothing.

"I regard sleep as a surrender," I said.

"Quiet now," she said.

•

Meanwhile, behind Jefferson Library, a car backing up threw red light on the iron palings, and the shadow of a bicycle was ridden across them, projected by headlights from West 10th.

•

In gym news, Skeezix, the world's foremost authority, has affected a beard and a pair of thick-framed glasses, which he whips off when making a point, like a news anchor, or when going off script, dilating on a topic, like a lecturer. I'm told he interrupted a recent tai chi class, his first, to give the teacher the benefit of his knowledge. Everyone gives him a wide berth. He's the only one on the kibitz bikes now. So he has to shout from his bike to a woman across the room to relay his impressions of a *New Yorker* piece. Glasses in hand. Through Zeppelin I can hear him.

"Congenital educator," I tell Lou on my way out.

"Ugh. He's got logorrhea, this guy. He's got the *malad'*. The only way he stops talking is when—" Lou puts a gun finger to his head and clicks his thumb.

•

Full moon, 4:30 a.m., 39 degrees, steam coming on. I'm over here and you're over there.

•

"You can never die. That's the one thing. You can. Never. Die. Do you hear me? Michael. You can't get hit by any cars or buses or taxis. You have to hold on to the rail so you don't fall overboard. You have to wear a seat belt at all times. You have to keep your hands inside the vehicle while it's moving, so you can't get swept away."

•

From the inbound B on the Manhattan Bridge, the outbound train is a blur through which I can see, in pinpoints of light, the outline of the Brooklyn Bridge.

Willie's back, for now. I see him from behind, skeletal, shorn, limping up the aisle with a cane and some sort of torso brace that looks like an exoskeleton.

"Willie! Welcome back!"

He turns. "*My* man."

"Good to see you."

"I know."

"Everybody's been asking about you. It must feel good to be back here."

"Shit yeah, baby."

•

Still dark out. She rolls over with her eyes closed and says "You're my bunny."

"Yeah."

". . ."

". . ."

"We're not waking up yet," she says. "Go back to sleep, Michael."

•

Four a.m. I can see red exit signs on three dark floors of a building a block east and two blocks north.

•

Get up to piss, I'm wobbly on my knees. Sharp pain from running yesterday. The bathroom's black, but there's another dimension in the mirror. A red pinpoint from the bedroom or somewhere out there in the city. I find the seat to lift it. I used to see better in the dark. Even a few years ago. I hate the idea that one day I might have to know the world by habit. I go back to bed dreading that we won't be able to look after each other. She's curled up, turned away from me in a short white flounce of nightgown, fearless. The alarm wakes me at five.

•

Two fifteen in the morning I was awake. Warily, she reached across and laid a finger on my right eye.

"What the hell are you doing?"

"I'm trying to see if you're awake."

"Next time just ask."

"Why are you awake?"

"I dunno, why are you awake?"

"What are you thinking about?"

"Nothing."

"You're worried about something."

"No."

"What is it?"

"I'm not worried, I promise."

"Tell me."

"Actually, I was just thinking about all these old Italian places I've been to in the boroughs."

"How many did you come up with?"

"Oh, I dunno. I wasn't counting."

"Do you want to list them?" she says, turning over and pushing onto my chest.

"No, that's okay."

"Go 'head, honey," she said, settling in. "What are they?"

"Well, Dominick's, of course, and Roberto's, in the Bronx. On Arthur Avenue. And another place up there, F and J Pine. In Brooklyn, there's Bamonte's and the Frost Restaurant, in Williamsburg. Queen, on Court Street, and Sam's, farther out on Court. Ferdinando's, in Red Hook. Monte's, in Gowanus; Two Toms, in Park Slope, where I was the only one there who didn't feel free to go into the kitchen, open the fridge, go behind the counter and make a call. Michael's, in Midwood. There's Randazzo's, in Sheepshead Bay . . ."

She was breathing more heavily now.

"Joe's of Avenue U, Gravesend, and L and B Spumoni Garden around the corner. New Corner, in Dyker Heights; Il Colosseo and La Palina, in Bensonhurst. Gargiulo's, in Coney Island."

She was fast asleep.

"In Queens," I went on, idiotically, "there's Manducatis, in Long Island City, and Piccola Venezia, in Astoria. Park Side, in Corona; Lenny's Clam Bar and Bruno, Howard Beach; Don Pepe, in Ozone Park . . ."

•

For Lou's birthday, I take him a container of chickpea soup out of the freezer, made with fennel and tomato and orange peel. We get talking about food.

"Our house used to smell so bad," he says. "My mother would fry cauliflower. Broccoli, smell up the whole house. Tripe, she made. Fish—forget about it."

"I remember that fish smell from my grandmother's place. Fish with garlic."

"Never get rid of it."

"No, because they lived upstairs in these airless—"

"Tenements, yeah. Or the sauce, on Sundays. On Sundays, every floor smelled different."

"I made braciole last week. That takes you back, the smell of that in the sauce."

"I used to like the rigatoni—with meatballs."

This gets us started on different approaches to the meatball. Two kinds of meat? Three? Or just beef. Ninety percent lean, or eighty/twenty? He holds the door for me as we go out in the cold, zips his hoodie, throws his scarf behind.

"Some people put raisins. And pignole."

"That must be Sicilian."

"Yeah. But I had it at a wiseguy's place in Queens— Punchy Illiano, part of the Gallo crew—he made it for me: delicious! I said 'How come you're making this? You're Napoletan.' He said 'I had them over a Sicilian's house and I liked 'em.' So he started making 'em like that himself."

•

The grey street-level air of a November afternoon. That grey of impending snow. The pavement seems to glow, and sounds are nearer. Somewhere a truck is backing up.

•

Saturday I walked over to my storage space. Manhattan Mini Storage, in a yellowbrick building takes up a whole block at the end of 17th Street, all the way west. Floor 10, aisle 7. Windowless quiet with the lights always on. A few of the aisles were taped off and there was a guy rolling a fresh coat of grey deck paint on the concrete floor. Big floor fan blowing to dry it.

Sign in the elevator:

> Holiday
> hours
> We will close
> at noon on
> Thanksgiving day
> and Christmas day,
> and will re-open
> the following
> mornings at 7am.

•

She turned to look at 14th Street through the reflection in the bus window, slipped a hand in mine, gave it a squeeze.

•

THE JUNE AND JANE SHOW

We're sitting in Elephant & Castle, where, amid the clatter of forks and dishes, Jane's talking about a long-ago Thanksgiving dinner . . .

JANE: —Because June always has to know what's going on. And you know how small my kitchen is.

MIKE: Yeah. One person at a time.

JANE: But she has to lift every lid, read all the ingredients, especially the tiniest print, to make sure there's no—

JUNE: Michael that doesn't happen. I was very young.

JANE: Uh-ha.

JUNE: I've evolved.

JANE: The expiration date, country of origin. She has to make sure you're not adding something she doesn't wanna eat. Always.

JUNE: Because she does.

JANE: No. Not on your plate.

JUNE: On everyone else's but mine? She'd say to me "Don't tell Sharon, but I did use butter. I didn't use olive oil, I used butter." So that's why I was in her kitchen looking in her pots making sure she wasn't sneaking any bacon—

JANE: I didn't!

JUNE: Or giblets, or other organ meats.

JANE: The *pupik*, maybe.

MIKE: Where is the *pupik* again, exactly?

JANE: And a touch of ground lungs.

MIKE: What were you making?

JANE: Stuffing. And I was using things she decided she couldn't eat at the time. 'Cause she's a vegetarian? And I was using chicken soup. But she didn't eat chicken soup, so I got vegetable broth and I made two pots of stuffing: one here and one there. She comes over and she starts to—wants to look at all the cans, in the garbage, and wrappers—"What's going on?"—she likes to ask a million things, she likes to poke around, she likes to get a spoon—she likes to do everything.

JUNE: You're exaggerating.

JANE: No, I'm not. All of a sudden, June is holding up this huge big bowl of stuffing—drops the whole thing upside down on the floor. "Oops!"

JUNE: [*Laughter*]

MIKE: And what'd you say?

JUNE: She told me to get the fuck out of her kitchen. "Get outa my house, get outa my kitchen!"

JANE: "Don't come back. I'll call *you*."

JUNE: "You're eating it."

JANE: *Annoying* is not the word.

•

Still dark when I go down the subway stairs in Brooklyn. I come up at Sixth Avenue to a grey-on-grey morning with an edge to the atmosphere, the thought of snow on the air. Lou's coming from the Y, I hand him five copies of *Travel + Leisure* in a brown paper bag, which he takes without breaking stride.

Behind me, someone says "What just happened?"

I do my workout. Before I go back down at Seventh, I stop at the top of the stairs to do the crosswords with Lenny. We talk about old movies and I give him a crime novel I'm done with.

"You going somewhere for Thanksgiving?" I ask him.

"I'll probably take it easy," he says. "Stay home and make some phone calls. I got a sister in New Jersey and a daughter down South. Then go to the Salvation Army. They serve Thanksgiving dinner in the afternoon. Beautiful dinner with turkey and all the fixings, very nice."

This used to be Steve's post, outside Duane Reade. We talked nearly every morning. One day Steve was gone, and a week later, Lenny was here.

•

It's dawn at the end of East 4th Street, at the end of Houston, the end of Delancey. The Williamsburg Bridge affords a view of dawn over the boroughs. Beside us, a bouncing dump truck sounds like the world hit its head on the roof. There's a cardboard pine tree swinging from the mirror, and LaGuardia's the usual mess.

•

Three p.m., finishing the dishes after Thanksgiving dinner with my mother, then we'll take a plate to my aunt at the nursing home. Back in New York, June's making a pie to take over to Jane's tonight. She sends an email: "I miss you so much that I am going to put on all your clothes and walk around the apartment, and maybe I'll go downstairs to the Westside Market in them too."

•

Four forty-five, very dark. I say her name, and within that syllable, the room just-perceptibly lightens. Yesterday was another rainy drive to Calvary. Goose tracks in the snow on my father's grave. And now I'm staring out at the luggage carts. Transparent shadow of a water bottle in a sunsplash on a seat back. How do we stand it, the tragedy of time always slipping through our fingers? This anticipation, the time we'll spend together this weekend—this is literally what we are, and we're losing it by the second. And now we roll back, and the frozen puddles and the wet tire tracks go orange.

•

I was cutting garlic in the kitchen. "Deeper Shade of Soul" came on. I popped my head out to say something and June was

dancing in her corner of the couch. I mean, it was minimal—
she was giving it as little as she could. A seated Canarsie: the
face of unconcern, hands overhead, keeping time. *Bugalú*—it's
irresistible, that beat. So then I started up with a kind of Egyp-
tian shuffle, side to side, head in profile, elbows at angles, like
a hieroglyph come to life on the wall of a tomb. She had her
arms up, phone in one hand, pointing this way, then that, still
not remotely bothered, and I was doing the Johnny Boy dance
that Robert De Niro does at the end of *Mean Streets*: hands
like twin pistols, side to side and up and back . . .

•

Lou's reading the paper on the treadmill, I stop to say hi.

"What's doing?" he says.

"I read an article this morning says that according to
sixty studies, exercise is worthless for weight loss."

"Nah, it does nothing," he says. "I been on here an hour
and a half. Whatever I burn, it's a slice of pizza. One ice-
cream cone. The only exercise that works is this—" and he
pantomimes pushing himself back from a table.

I said "You know what I really miss about being young?
It isn't drinking or smoking or whatever, it's doing what I
want and not worrying about it. Like you're gonna live forever. You get older and no matter what you do you see shadows in the corner."

"That's right. But your father went, right?"

"Yeah, he did."

"So you're gonna go too. Nothing you can do about it. You know what this guy told me once? Joe Beck, a bookmaker—he was half a gangster, bookie—he started drinking, wife threw him out, his daughter didn't have nothing to do with him: all kinda problems. He had money, but nothing to live for. So he told me 'I don't care what happens to me, I'm ready. I'm ready to go.' I said 'What, you wanna die?' He said 'Hey, if it was good enough for Al Capone.'"

•

At dawn I'm walking through Tompkins Square Park. Sound of geese overhead like the sound of fucking on old bedsprings.

•

June and I went crunching through the crusted snow to the lake, late in the afternoon. Wet tracks—from people, deer, small animals—had exposed the grass underneath. We made our way through dry dead weeds. The lake was still. No breeze, nothing moving. I smelled the mud and wet snow and felt I'd let my most vital connection lapse, and for so long it could never be made right. Taken a wrong turn a long time ago. Living in the city, you forget you're going to die. But I remembered that kind of afternoon—the white snow against the dark-grey sky—like I remembered my death. It rang a bell.

•

I was at the wheel, driving us across Pennsylvania, back to New York. She'd been asleep for an hour.

I slowed us onto an exit ramp and she opened her eyes. She said "What else, Bunny?"

So foggy you can't see the corner. But when you get there, there's no fog there. It's at the next corner. And behind you. It's the illusion of density. Of substance. It's the buildings uptown disappearing behind screens of snow that don't exist at any point between here and there. It's that one December, seen through layers of subsequent Decembers and backed by Decembers that came before it. On the ground, that December had no apparent mood or hue or characteristics, there was no thingness to it. Its qualities are apparent only from here, looking back.

When was there ever more than a moment's perch in time?

•

One night after work, forty years ago, in Cleveland, I took the Rapid Transit train downtown, a Friday night in early December, that's how I remember it, right after work, in the dark. For some reason, maybe by mistake, I took the train to 25th Street instead of downtown. I was going to the record store, Record Rendezvous, where Jimmy Jones presided, maybe it was payday, and after mentally paying all my bills and figuring and refiguring my budget for the next two weeks, maybe I had an extra twenty to blow. I could usually manage to buy a record or two every couple of weeks. Anyway, I got off the Rapid at this deserted station, this deserted platform across the river from downtown, and it was snowing. I was a little lost but not completely lost, because I could see the Terminal Tower across the river, through the falling snow. I was just lost enough. And since I had nowhere to be that night and didn't have to work the next day, which opened my imagination or dropped my defenses against it, and since I was accountable to no one, I started walking toward downtown. I must have dared myself to do it—*just walk there*—and started walking down the hill toward the river. Not that it was a long walk or anything. It was a challenge to routine, to the idea that I had to get right home or explain myself to anyone or to myself. It was a challenge to established routes. And so I made my way downhill and then, in the dark among the weeds, I found an unused road along the river, and I followed it. The snow was falling in big flakes and ticking into the weeds, and through it I could still see the Terminal Tower. I was lost but not too lost, and because it was Friday and payday I was free, but just free enough to know it. I think of this as the time of *Sandinista!*, the Clash record, but it could have been a year later. I don't remember what I bought at the record store, I don't remember being there, I don't remember downtown or by what bridge I crossed the river. What I remember is walking on a road that wasn't quite a road, through tall dead weeds, with the Terminal Tower visible through the falling snow, in the early dark of a Friday in December, having what turns out to have been one of the happiest nights of my life.

•

"Yeah, Mike. This is Lou, I got your message. I'll call you later. To figure out what to do. It's no big deal. Y'know, there's no rush. The only problem is tomorrow—I gotta leave the gym early. By eight, I gotta be out. Eight thirty, the latest. Eight fifteen, the latest, 'cause I gotta go to the fur market. Give this guy a hand. He called me, says 'Lou, you come in, I need you for, y'know, just for the day.' I'll probably work about, who knows, ten hours, twelve hours. But he takes care of me pretty good. So, uh—anyway . . . I'll call you later, we'll figure it out—maybe you can leave them in the building, or whatever. Alright? But no pressure. And, ah— those cookies from Fortunato's were *delicious*. The filled one I liked—What was that, a *pasta ciotta*. The one with the ricot' inside's *delicious*. Had it with coffee. Alright. —Even the biscotti: *delicious.* I thought they were there longer than that, 1976. Alright. Later. I'll be in touch."

●

I step out of the YMCA but the day outside is just a larger room. One of those days the sun never quite comes up, and it's getting dark already at eight a.m. Down the end of 14th Street, bare branches have stained the white sky pink around the edges. It's a card you mailed in childhood that dropped in your box today.

●

On the kitchen counter, I filled a big glass jar with a pound of ground Italian espresso roast from Porto Rico. I moved a half-pound bar of Irish butter from the freezer to the butter compartment. Also in the fridge, by way of staples, were a carton of eggs, a jar of grated Locatelli, and a Tupperware cylinder where I collected Parmesan rinds, which I used in soup. The freezer had a loaf of rye, half a loaf of raisin bread, and provisions diverted from dinners I'd made: beef borscht, chickpea soup, and sauce with braciole and sausage. In a blue ceramic bowl on the counter were a bulb and a half of garlic, and beside the sink bottles of vinegar and a liter of oil, nearly full. In the cabinet, there were open and unopened boxes of linguine, capellini, and farfalle. So we were pretty well fixed.

•

She's away, and the bed feels like there's no one in it, not even me. The Empire State Building stands there breathing cold white light in the fog like an organ not of sound but of light: dimming, disappearing . . . brightening to upthrust white light of the 1930s before dimming again . . . disappearing . . . until there's only that diamond cat collar above the moving clouds.

•

On my way through the cardio room, I stop to see Lou. He's on a stair machine, he's been there an hour, reading the papers, climbing. He gives me some newspaper items he's been saving for me. An obituary. A piece about a new health study that debunks an old one. A supermarket circular where he points out a couple of specials.

Philly's on a rowing machine. I ask him how it's going.

"I'm depressed," he says. "Time of year. I'm getting old. I turned seventy the other day!"

"Yeah, it's the holidays. Maybe the new year things turn around for you. Maybe you meet a girlfriend."

"I had a girlfriend. She moved to Arizona."

"I remember."

"Broke my heart. That's been five years now. I don't think that's gonna happen for me anymore."

He takes a good pull.

Then he looks up and says "What's gonna happen to me, Mikey? I got old."

"Anything can happen anytime."

"I used to think that."

"Don't give up hope. Because you know what the alternative is?"

"What's that?"

"You start keeping an eye on the price of rib roast, like Lou. He just gave me an ad for Stew Leonard."

"You're right, pal."

•

Waiting behind a dirty windshield on Kenmare Street. There's red light caught in the grain of the road and in the steam rising from an exhaust pipe. Just waiting, in this *heat* of consciousness I call my life. Right now is where it hurts to miss you: the parts I know I won't remember. This is where real life is: down in the folds of time's fan. Then the steam turns green.

•

Lying awake in the dark . . . a nerve in the night . . . feeling that she and I are mortal and vulnerable and there's not much standing between us and old age . . . a siren goes by . . . in that bath of night that isn't really dark . . . where the room and what's in it are a pointillation of grey and orange and lilac . . . and even the black windows in the wall outside are seen as if through snow . . . that familiar noncolor of night in every city, all your life . . . a "darkness" that doesn't hide you. There's no safety in the dark. There isn't even much darkness in it.

•

Snowcapped water towers emerging in the blue hour. Caillebotte.

•

sirens gossiping down Seventh Avenue in the night

•

Today I was bitching to Lou about this guy Marvin, who started out with a padlock on one of the public lockers for weeks on end and who's now got four lockers tied up with his dry cleaning and shampoos and ointments and ramen and depositions and accordion files and who knows what, running some kind of whizbang law practice out of the locker room. "It's getting to be I can't find a locker in the morning, with this guy."

Lou says "Mike, ya gotta realize. These guys are up against it, some of them. What if it was you, living like this? Where's your *rachmanis*?"

•

Sunday I'm reading on the bed. In our neighbor's window the water towers are stacked in a lemongrey sky. All day the light doesn't change. All day a teakettle wind is whistling in the vents and the white slow plumes of steam are rising. All day I'm here reading—how many of these days do you get in a year? In a lifetime? Late in the afternoon the sun comes out. And then the light gets dialed down and dialed down until, in a deep-blue sky, only a few silver rooftop pipes are still gleaming. Dialed down until there's one white water tower bobbing on a sea of night that's poured into the streets below, and those rooftop pipes are the gold of smoked sable.

•

I woke to the sound of a shovel scraping the sidewalk below. Last night, I walked her to the subway in a blizzard, which was also the year's first snowfall. Snowswirl. It snowed upward, it spiraled down the side streets, hit you broadside at the intersections. Someone was laughing but you couldn't look up. Then *she* was laughing, standing in a drift. She stopped walking and just let it go, like we were standing in a rowboat that was going down in three feet of water and it was the funniest thing ever. She was able to laugh at herself. And in that laughter I heard all of life, why we live, even though we suffer and even though we die, why it's still worth it. Headlights floated by. A tall young guy fell in step with us. He was holding the remains of an umbrella over his head. He looked like he'd walked out of a Roadrunner cartoon. He asked where we were going. When we crossed the road to drop off a movie I said "You're on your own!" We heard him through the snow, looking for a new friend. He didn't seem to have seen snow before. She said "He must be from California." I missed her even with her at my side. She'd turned me inside out. Or I'd done it for her. I felt as though my heart was on the outside, beating. There was never enough of her. I could never get close enough, never possess her completely enough. As though there were some measure of completeness beyond complete, something beyond now, something in the realm of the imagination, some essence. I felt as though maybe cannibalism was the answer.

To kill and eat her right there in the snow. She claimed to feel exactly the same, but it's hard to know. I kissed her at the subway, she was just a nose and a smile encircled by a snowy hood. I told her to hold the rail and watched her down.

The walk home was desolate. Outside my hood was near silence. Except for a plastic tarp on a motorcycle snapping in the wind. By the time I made it to my building, my coat and scarf were white. I waited for the elevator with the snow melting off me, missing her something terrible. Inside my apartment, I locked the door, as though protecting what remained of her presence there. The screens were clotted with snow and there were five inches of it on the outside sill. I hung my scarf and coat and gloves in the shower, dried my hair with a towel, and went to bed listening to the radiator, with the room cast in orange snowlight.

And this morning I lay there listening to that shovel scrape the sidewalk, and then silence. My heart was still on the outside, beating, waiting.

•

Through two jogging sets of smeary windows: a woman in a white ski jacket, far end of the next car, which swung out to one side, ahead us on the curve. Her face was turned away. The lights went out and then back on.

Monday I walked past Lou at his locker.

"I didn't see you this weekend," he said. "You were here?"

"I was here yesterday. Night we stayed home."

"You cooked?"

"I made pasta with garlic and oil."

"What'd you do?"

I went back to him. I said "My friend Tammy gave me a truffle slicer. I used it for the garlic. Red pepper flakes."

"Parsley?" he said.

"Yeah, parsley, at the end, with lemon."

"Romano?"

"I used Parmesan last night. What about you?" I said.

"Same thing. I made pasta with garlic and oil. I ate the whole pound."

"You ate a *pound* of linguine?"

"I used the vermicelli."

"I haven't had that in a long time. De Cecco?"

"Ronzoni," he said. "It was on sale, three pounds for two dollars."

Now Painter Joe was there. He was unwinding his wraps and hanging them in his locker. Yesterday he told us about the Lanzetti brothers, from South Philly: six brothers, five named after popes. All gangsters. Pius, Leo, Teo, Lucien, Ignatius, and Willie—all mob guys.

He said "You gotta reserve a cup of the pasta water."

Lou said "How about linguine fini? Ever use that?"

"I made it the other night," I said.

"Garlic and oil?"

"Yeah. And breadcrumbs, I made."

This opened a discussion of different techniques for linguine with garlic and oil. Painter Joe, in a jockstrap, said he uses a couple of anchovies. A man drying his balls down the aisle said he adds a squeeze of lemon. Lou tucked his shirt in and squatted to settle into his pants. He doesn't sauté his garlic, he throws it in fresh at the end.

"There's always something else," I said. "You're never done, with pasta."

"A continuing fascination," Lou said. He was combing his hair in the mirror. "You're never done."

•

By the time I got on the treadmill, the sun had shot below the clouds and raised every ridge and bump on 14th Street, each with its own shadow, including a tall slant beside the Salvation Army sign. She'd been living at Jane's for a few months, but she still couldn't see her way clear to saying what she wanted, and my head was still full of the stuff I came to the Y to outrun. The past, the future. The guys she'd been with and what was going to be with us.

With the iPod on shuffle I was going pretty good when up chimed an acoustic guitar, a twelve-string, ringing and droning around me as though I were inside the instrument. Whoever it was took two deliberate, formal passes at a theme, and then played that same theme at a clip. First the shadow, then the sun. Perfect simple thing. I looked at the device: Leo Kottke, "In Christ There Is No East or West." Still running, I played it again. First the ceremony, then the dance. All the same tune. In our circle there's no east or west or north or south. No future or past, no yours or mine, no me or you. There's only us and only now. And if we can stay here, it'll always be now, and if it's always now, we can stay.

And then it's the Allmans playing "Jessica" and I'm still running, happy and suddenly free, opening it up like they do, with a blind cloud of sunlight at the windows. Nothing in front of me and nothing behind. Tomorrow's just another today. And I don't have to undo the knots and unfasten the locks and retrace the routes and mazes that led me to a moment's peace yesterday. All I have to do is accept today's joy.

Once in a while you see through "time."

And then it was pavement grey out there again. Behind the pebbled glass, someone stopped to light a cigarette in cupped hands and the red strobe of an ambulance moving panel to panel threw his shadow on the glass.

I was out of the shower by 8:25, drying off. She was meeting me at 8:30. All I had to do is get dressed and she'd be there, on the other side of this moment, like the other side of a door.

I went upstairs. Outside, a few snowflakes were in the air, small ones. Schoolkids were shrieking all around me. A voice told me *Look around. You won't be here again.*

June was crossing Sixth Avenue. She was coming past the newsstand. It seemed there was barely time left for us. And then she was right in front of me. To me, she looked like she did when she was 27. Maybe to her, I did too. That's the thing about being with someone who knew you when you were young: she'll always see you that way.

She was standing close. As close as people do in the movies. Her green eyes were studying mine. She must have seen something.

"Don't say anything," she said.

Another ambulance was going by. I was looking at her hair.

I turned up her collar.

"Zip up," I said.

Acknowledgments

Yuka Igarashi is the reason you're reading this: she brought this book in from the cold. In the happy event the publication of *Jacket Weather* comes to seem as if it was inevitable, I'll know otherwise. That it should have found her seems a miracle to me, even if it's one with an easy explanation: Steve Levine and Chris Kraus, to both of whom I'm forever grateful. Max Blagg and Danielle Leone kept the wind in my sails. Sally DeCapite has done that for nearly six decades. Wah-Ming Chang prepared the text for print with incredible care and precision, and Michael Salu gave me the perfect cover. Really, it's been a too-brief pleasure to work with everyone I've met at Soft Skull. And each of the following people helped in some way: Sanjay Agnihotri, Cindy Barber, Ted Barron, Sheelagh Bevan, Laura Blackburn, Vince Bruner, Suzanne DeGaetano, Maggie Dubris, Jane Friedman, Robert Gordon, Rebecca Gowen, Philly Grossman, BG

Hacker, Ray Halliday, Richard Hell, Clinton Heylin, Greg Jiritano, Mimi Lipson, Tony Maimone, Greg Masters, Brian S. McGrath, Joel Murach, Elinor Nauen, Will Patton, Heather Price-Wright, Rosa Ransom, Kelly Reichardt, Luc Sante, Joe Santore, Mark Satlof, Tere Saylor, Pete Simonelli, Anna van der Meulen, and Jocko Weyland. I'm very happy to thank Nile Butta, who reintroduced me to June. And above all June, my feelings for whom I've spent an entire novel trying to encompass, and now I've run out of room.

© Ted Barron

Under the banner of Sparkle Street Books, MIKE DECAPITE has published the novel *Through the Windshield*, the chapbook *Creamsicle Blue*, and the short-prose collection *Radiant Fog*. Cuz Editions published his story "Sitting Pretty," later anthologized in *The Italian American Reader*. DeCapite lives in New York City.